SNOW & ROSE

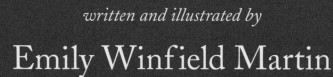

written and illustrated by

Emily Winfield Martin

SNOW

&

ROSE

Random House 🏠 New York

First Printing

𝓔𝓌𝓂

Copyright © 2017 by Emily Winfield Martin

All rights reserved. Published in the United States by
Random House Children's Books, a division of
Penguin Random House LLC, New York.

Random House and the colophon are registered trademarks of
Penguin Random House LLC.

Visit us on the Web! randomhousekids.com

Educators and librarians, for a variety of teaching tools, visit us at
RHTeachersLibrarians.com

Library of Congress Cataloging-in-Publication Data
is available upon request.

ISBN 978-0-553-53818-2 (trade) —
ISBN 978-0-553-53819-9 (lib. bdg.) — ISBN 978-0-553-53820-5 (ebook)

MANUFACTURED IN CHINA
10 9 8 7 6 5 4 3 2 1
First Edition

To my mother,
who called me Rose Red

CONTENTS

CHAPTER 1
Snow and Rose

Once, there were two sisters.

Rose had hair like threads of black silk and cheeks like two red petals and a voice that was gentle and sometimes hard to hear. Snow had hair like white swan down and eyes the color of the winter sky, with a laugh that was sudden and wild.

They lived in a cottage in the woods, but it hadn't always been so.

"Tell me a story," Snow called in the dark. She moved restlessly, wide awake in her bed.

"You'll wake Mama," Rose murmured. "Go back to sleep."

Snow sat up, her bed creaking. "Rose?" Her whisper drifted in the dark. "Please?"

Their bedroom was a loft that lay above the hearth and kitchen and below a pointed ceiling. On one side were the sisters' beds. On the other side was their mother's bed. Rose peered through the gap in the faded screen that turned one small room into two very tiny ones. The blue light in the window showed the curve of their mother's side rising and falling softly.

Rose sighed. "Okay, but I'll come over there." The hush of a match sounded as Rose lit the yellow beeswax stump between their beds, followed by a few soft tiptoed thumps as her feet padded across the floor. She climbed under the covers of Snow's bed.

"Your feet are freezing," Snow whispered.

Rose drew her knees up to her chest. "Which story do you want to hear?" Rose asked. Her dark hair glowed with glints of red and gold in the candle's light. "The one about the magic lamp?"

"No," Snow said, pulling the covers tightly around her shoulders. She smiled, her pale hair a messy tumble on the pillow.

"The mermaid and the monkey?" Rose asked.

"No," Snow whispered impatiently. "Not that one."

"Or the fairy tale about—"

"No, no fairy tales." Snow tugged gently on the sleeve of Rose's nightgown. "Tell the story of us."

After another sigh, Rose began.

"Once upon a time," Rose whispered in her best storyteller's voice, "there were two girls, one with black hair and one with white. They were born to a nobleman who was as tall and as broad as he was gentle and kind. Their mother was from a common family, but she had a rare and delicate beauty, like—"

"Like a Siamese cat," Snow offered.

"Yes, like a Siamese cat," Rose continued softly. "And their mother was a painter and sculptor, who loved to wake up the things she said were asleep inside big slabs of marble, and her statues filled the sculpture garden. And their father loved to build places that didn't exist until he imagined them. He loved to read about all the things that other people had imagined and built, so he had a library with shelves that reached to the ceiling.

"Their mother and father loved each other, too, of course, more than books or sculptures. But more than anything else, they loved their two daughters.

"And since love is something you cannot see, the mother and father tried their best to make an invisible thing visible. So when the girls were both still very small, their parents commissioned a spectacular garden, a wonder that people would come from miles and miles to see. Stretching the entire length of the house, this garden was like no garden that had ever existed or will ever exist again.

"Half of the garden was filled entirely with white flowers of every kind—with pale, delicate bells of lily of the valley, spires of vanilla foxgloves with speckled throats, climbing moonflower vines, and bright-eyed anemones, from the tiniest white daisy to ivory dahlias the size of dinner plates. And—"

"And it was called the Snow Garden," Snow interrupted.

"And it was called the Snow Garden," repeated Rose with a sad smile. "And the other half bloomed only in red: vermilion poppies and scarlet pansies and wine-colored snapdragons and Japanese lanterns the color of fire. And dozens and dozens of roses, each with a hundred red petals . . ."

Rose trailed off. She knew hearing the story made Snow happy; otherwise she wouldn't ask for it all the time. But for Rose, in the telling of it, she was left with a hollow that grew with each word.

Rose knew her sister was the kind of person who wanted to see or hear or taste something she loved over and over again, to remind herself that it was real. Rose was another kind of person: she wanted to hold on to a thing she loved as tightly as she could. She wanted to keep it special and safe, for fear that it might get used up—or worse, that it might escape, like sand or sugar slipping between her fingers.

"You know a lot of words for *red,*" Snow whispered. Her eyes were closed. "Now tell about the swans."

Rose looked at her sister's face, a content pale moon in the dark.

Rose breathed in and pulled the quilt to her chest. She continued the story dutifully, her voice as low as she could make it, so low it was barely there. "And in the center of the Snow Garden and the Rose Garden was a pond ringed with willows, and tracing circles on the water were two swans, one white with a dark golden beak, and the other coal black with a beak of the brightest red.

"And this is where the girls were born, the place they grew up. This is where they had closets stuffed with dozens of beautiful dresses, where their porcelain dolls had so many lovely things to wear they needed closets of their own. This is where they had an extremely fat cat named Earl Grey, and where they had their lessons and acted out plays and had their tea. And when they played hide-and-seek, Snow would always hide in the sculpture garden and Rose would always hide in the library, so it wasn't even that good a game. . . ."

Rose looked down to see if Snow was awake. Her sister's eyelids fluttered, but she didn't seem to notice that the story had stopped.

Rose went on, her voice even softer than before, as quiet as a breath. "And at night, this is where they were tucked into big brass beds wrought with flowers and birds, and where their father would read them to sleep or tell them stories about magic lamps and dragons and faraway places. . . ."

Gently, Rose climbed out of the warm covers and tucked them around Snow's shoulders. "As their mother put out the lights, their father would say, 'Go to sleep, my only Snow. Go to sleep, my only Rose.'"

She made her way back to her own bed and snuffed out the candle.

"The end."

X X X

But that wasn't *really* the end.

There was more, but it wasn't the kind of story anyone wants to tell, let alone call their story, because it was full of tears, and horses who can't speak, and fathers who never come home, and questions that have no answers.

The simplest version was this: Their father had set out one day into the woods and never returned. His horse had come back alone, the only witness to what had happened. When their mother opened the bag that hung at the horse's side, and spread the contents on the ground, their father's things seemed to be untouched. His ledgers, his pipe and tobacco, and even a fold of paper money were all there. Only three things were missing: a watch, a blanket, and a knife.

These weren't clues that meant anything, really. They could be wherever he was, these things. The girls hoped he was somewhere, anywhere. He might return, might fling open the doors with a wild story to tell. He might.

But the day after the horse came home, the sisters overheard the cooks whispering. Snow and Rose stood around the corner, holding their breath as the cooks chattered in speculation: "A dozen things could've done him in: great beasts . . . old enchantments . . . Menace of the Woods . . . or the Bandits of No Man's Land. . . . A dozen things . . . and the poor little misses will never know. . . ."

Every whisper that filled the air in that house was the same: since there were wild things in the forest, something wild had been the death of him.

Still, for days, they hoped. Rose and Snow wandered the halls of the echoing house they lived in then, half expecting to see him or hear his voice. It was hard to believe that a person could be there and then suddenly *not* be there, never be there. So the sisters waited and watched. But the more days that passed, the more a final, terrible truth settled in the air.

That was when their mother locked herself in her room. That was when Rose holed up in the library and cried herself to sleep in the chair her father used to sit in when they read together. She fell asleep wishing the truth to be something else. But every time she woke up, the truth was still there.

But Snow didn't cry, not even then. She didn't cry because the truth everyone else felt was *not* her truth. She wouldn't believe her father was gone. And no matter how much time passed, she insisted he would come back. Rose couldn't say to Snow, to insist to *her*, that sometimes you lose someone in a way that means he will never read to you, or say good night, or swing his arms around you again.

The servants dyed a few of the girls' dresses black, and this was what they wore, day after day. It wasn't long after they put on their black dresses that the man with the thin face came. The sisters watched as he told their mother that they couldn't live in the house with the Snow Garden and the Rose Garden anymore. He told her that the gardens and the house and the dresses and the library and the servants and all the rest belonged to the council of noble families.

That was when Snow kicked the man with the thin face soundly in the shins, but it didn't change what they had to do.

They left the house and went to a cottage in the woods, the woods that had stolen their father and husband, the woods that people whispered about in tales of strange and wild things. They went to the woods because there was nowhere else to go.

And the ending of *that* story is the beginning of this story.

Snow and Rose didn't know they were living in a fairy tale—people never do.

x x x

They came to the cottage when spring was nearly summer. Snow, Rose, and their mother brought with them enough to make a new life in the woods, including Earl Grey, squirming in Snow's arms. To get there, one simply followed the path, which began at the edge of the woods, high on the hillside. There could be no confusion because there was only one path, one way through the forest. It wasn't a real road but one cleared by feet and wheels and hooves.

The cottage was made of stone and wood, and sat alone in the forest. It had belonged to their mother's great-uncle, who had built it when he was a young man,

a long time ago. She had visited him there when she was almost too small to remember, called Edie instead of Edith.

Snow and Rose didn't know of its existence until it became their home, and by then it had been empty for so long that the stone outside was furred in moss and the inside was blanketed in dust and strung with cobwebs. When they arrived and were standing just inside the door, their mother put her hands on her daughters' shoulders and gave them each a small squeeze that meant, *I cannot do this alone.*

So for the first time in their lives, the girls had to clean. They cleaned out the tin shed and pulled water from the well and scrubbed the cottage from the tops of the walls to the floorboards, pulling long-abandoned birds' nests from the fireplace. They helped their mother stuff mattresses for the three beds and fill the pantry with the cartload the cooks had sent with them, sacks of flour and grains and coffee and sugar.

All that remained of their old life fit into three trunks. When they had unpacked the useful and ordinary things, like clothes and pots and quilts, and their mother had hung their father's portrait on the wall, Snow and Rose found their special box. It was nestled in the bottom of the last trunk. It held their treasures. Inside was Snow's violin, which she placed carefully on a shelf next to her bed, not knowing if she'd ever feel like playing it again. The other treasures were the gifts their father brought them from his travels: a quilt from Bengal that was sewn together with ten thousand stitches, a book of stories from Japan, a little Turkish carpet, a brass elephant from Africa.

When the cottage was clean and the trunks were unpacked, the family began to find a routine in an unfamiliar place. But something else was unfamiliar to Snow and Rose. Their mother never smiled. She didn't paint or carve or do anything she used to do. She drifted through the house like a sleepwalker, her movements and conversations automatic and distant. She was more delicate than ever, but her sadness hung around her heavily. It took up a lot of room in such a small house.

Since they did not know what to do, the sisters went outside. Snow and Rose would wake up and have their breakfast, and then Snow would walk down the path through the trees, step beyond the border of the woods, and watch their old house down in the valley.

Snow made it no secret that she didn't like the cottage. She didn't like the peasant stew or the rough bread they ate with it. She didn't like the hard beds or the drafts that whistled through the gaps in the walls at night. Snow didn't like it when Rose said, "It will get better." How could it? The cottage was small and shabby, and shabby things don't turn into something *better*.

Most of all, Snow didn't like the people who had moved into their old house. They had stolen her life and stolen their gardens. So all through the spring, she watched the house, with Earl Grey beside her. Together they watched the comings and goings of the invaders, like two hungry cats ready to pounce on unsuspecting prey.

While Snow watched their old house and seethed, Rose would nestle against a tree with a book or go for a walk with her satchel over her shoulder, up and down the path. Between Snow's anger and her mother's sadness, it was hard for Rose to keep her own heart afloat, but the walks helped. As she made notes of the ferns and flowers that grew at her feet, she strained her eyes to see what lay in the dark forest beyond the path, and for those moments her curiosity drowned out everything else. The path to the village was well traveled and bright. But after all they had heard, after all that had happened, Rose was careful not to leave the path.

Sometimes she would go find Snow on the hillside and read aloud beside her. Or weave wild flowers into chains, trying to soften the sharpness of Snow's anger.

Out on the hillside, where nobody but Earl Grey

could hear, the sisters whispered to each other. They wondered about the things that were missing when the horse came back alone. What they meant, if they were clues, if they were still somewhere in the woods. They wondered about the way the woods might take someone and why.

The wondering burned inside them both but took different shapes because of what they believed: Rose wanted to know why their father had been taken, and Snow wanted to know how to get him back. Their wondering touched the edges of things they could never know, about this place that had changed their fortunes once and would change them again.

WHAT THE TREES SAW

"It is happening," the young one said in a voice like rustling leaves.

"It is," said the old one.

> "One man falls in the black of night
> Two babes come
> One dark, one light
> The child will fall
> And the beast will roar
> And blood and gold will reign
> No more."

"I know the prophecy," the old one sighed.

"They are his daughters, the one who fell. The one who bled into the leaves," the young one said with certainty. "Yes, it is them."

"It is possible," the old one said, hushed even in their hidden place.

"They are the ones who will end it all," the young one said.

"But first, one of them will fall."

CHAPTER 2
The Heart of the Woods

On a summer morning when the air was already hot, Rose made up her mind. Snow couldn't spend all her days watching the old house. Though Snow was two years younger, Rose was embarrassed to be almost afraid of her sister. Rose pictured herself as a tidy bow, and Snow was a wild tangle. Rose straightened the braids that crowned her head as she walked down the path, toward the bright sun that already warmed her skin at the edges of the forest.

Rose found Snow on the hillside in a sea of high grass. Some people's worry lives in their clenched teeth or high shoulders. Rose's worry lived in her hands, and she clasped and unclasped her fingers now. She stepped closer and cleared her throat. "Snow."

Her sister turned around, startled.

Just then Rose saw a band of five men across the hillside. Dressed in dull colors, their worn jackets trimmed with rows of metal buttons, they looked like ramshackle soldiers. They stood a few hundred yards away to the west, their figures dark against the meadow. Their voices carried across the open air.

Snow pulled Rose down to where she and Earl Grey were half-hidden in the grass. "Well, what is it?" Snow asked.

Rose cocked her head toward the band of men. "What are you *doing*?" Rose whispered, her eyebrows knitted together. She looked at the men, and then back at her sister. Her eyes grew big. "Are those . . . ?" she asked, trailing away. Snow gave her an ominous look and nodded before Rose could finish. "The Bandits of No Man's Land?"

"I'm spying on them," Snow said in a hushed voice, sinking lower in the grass. "You remember what the cooks said. And what I want to know is—what are they doing on *our* hillside?"

"Well," Rose whispered, "if they don't belong any-where . . . I guess they could be *everywhere*."

The bandits were walking in their direction now.

Rose's own heart started beating faster. "We shouldn't be here."

Earl Grey bristled his back with a loud hiss, giving them away.

The men's voices suddenly grew quiet. The only sound they made was the rushing of their boots in the grass, growing closer and closer until they discovered the girls. "What's this?" one of the men called. "Two little girls from town?"

The girls froze in their hiding place. The cat hissed again, then bolted toward the woods.

"They must be far from home," said another, dressed in tattered gray. He eyed Rose's beautiful satchel, their fine shoes and delicate silk dresses. "Are you far from home, little misses?"

"Are *you*?" Snow asked, scowling at the men.

Rose gave Snow a sideways glance, then grabbed her hand. Rose didn't believe in impossible things, but she did believe in dangerous men. She jumped to her feet, pulling Snow up with her, and took off in a run.

The men followed close behind, taking strides so big in their tall boots that they hardly had to run to close the distance between themselves and the girls. The bandits grew closer, following the girls on the path that wound through the forest.

The sisters passed everything that looked familiar

at the edge of the woods, the bandits just behind them. "We have to leave the path," Rose said, out of breath. Snow looked at her and nodded.

The girls took a turn the path didn't take. They dashed through a bank of dark-leaved mountain laurel and into a dense thicket. Branches grabbed at their shoulders, and ferns whipped their legs. The sun fell in glittering bars as the leaves rustled overhead.

The trees ushered the girls along, deeper into the woods. Their swaying branches beckoned like arms, *This way,* farther from the path. Snow and Rose followed without knowing something led them. The forest is where things live that are as old as the world—the spirits within the trees, hidden from view. They see all that happens: the little and big, the lives and deaths, the comings and goings. The trees watched them now, the two girls who had come.

Finally, the girls' running slowed to a walk. Snow and Rose couldn't hear the men's voices or heavy footsteps anymore. The bandits hadn't left the road, because of something almost no one knew: they feared the deep woods. More than once, a brother left in the morning and never returned, risking danger for a promise that took him into the trees. So the bandits lived at the edges, specializing in strangers, travelers who had something worth taking. Where *they* were the risk and danger. The bandits knew what was worth their while, and it was rarely worth their while to venture into the heart of the woods.

X X X

The girls stopped and listened closely to be sure the men were gone. As they caught their breath, the sisters saw how deep into the woods they had run—into air that was cool and dark, where a carpet of moss stretched out before them and walls of unfamiliar trees towered around them. But they didn't turn back. They had left the path; there was no changing that.

Rose put on her sternest face and turned to Snow. "What were you *thinking?*"

"Maybe they know something about Papa," Snow replied, indignant.

"Maybe they *did* something to Papa!" Rose said. "And what do you think they would've done to us?"

But now that the men were gone, a part of Rose was happy. She could see what lay beyond the well-traveled path, and Snow was at her side. So they went on farther, leaving no footprints in the black forest floor.

"Do you want to go back?" Rose said, feeling a wisp of a worry.

Snow shook her head.

"Me neither." Rose squashed the worry before it grew. She could find their way back when it was time.

Snow pointed to the shadow of a bird, and the sisters watched as it glided between the treetops, graceful and weightless, turning from a shadow into a bird at least twice as big as an ordinary blackbird. From the ground, they could just make out a white patch on its chest.

Suddenly, the bird dove sharply, so low its wings grazed Rose's hair. Rose shrieked.

The bird shot away. The sound of wings, like black sails flapping, surrounded them, then disappeared as the bird vanished from sight.

"Was it trying to *get* me?" Rose's heart had barely slowed after their escape, and now it was racing again.

Snow laughed. "It was trying to get *these*." She ran

to a dense thicket of brambles that sloped ahead in a sunny patch.

Rose smoothed down her ruffled braids, then followed.

Snow picked ripe blue-black fruit from between rough leaves and thorns. "Who'd want to snarfle you up when there are blackberries to eat?"

They stained their hands and piled their pockets full. Out of the brambles, a brown bunny bounded by with three little ones close behind. Snow and Rose watched them dash into their burrow, the last thoughts of the bandits chased away.

The sun still poured through the trees, and the girls walked on, eating berries. Not far from the thicket, they heard the sound of water and followed it until they found a stream. They took off their shoes and socks and dangled their feet in the water, looking down through the sparkling surface at the smooth rocks and silver fish just below their toes.

Rose picked the miniature daisies beside the stream and braided a crown. After settling it on her own dark hair, she started one for Snow.

"This isn't so terrible, is it?" Rose's voice was quiet above the sound of the stream. She swirled her toe in the water.

"No, it's not," Snow said. "It's not so terrible."

Rose plunked the second crown of flowers on Snow's head. It was too big and fell to Snow's narrow shoulders like a necklace.

Snow raised an eyebrow and Rose laughed, lifting off the crown to fix it.

"I left the stems too long," Rose said. She adjusted the crown, and this time it perfectly encircled Snow's head.

Snow looked down at her legs doubled in the reflection of the river. "It's okay for now."

Rose hesitated. "But what if it is for longer than now?"

"When Papa comes back . . . you know . . ." Snow threw a rounded stone in, rippling the stream. "Then everything will go back to normal."

Rose jumped up. "I'll race you to the other side," she said, grabbing her shoes and hopping to a stone in the middle of the stream. Rose finished stepping across and pounced on the bank, and Snow followed after. Rose couldn't bring herself to say, *He's not coming back.*

They continued into the very heart of the forest, into a grove of the oldest-looking trees they'd ever seen. In big, untidy rows grew a gathering of hunched old men, with beards of gray-green lichen and roots that sprawled like ancient hands. The sun was lower in the sky now, and everything was dusted in a hazy glow. Little insects and bits of dust bobbed in the amber light around them. It was the time of day called the golden hour.

Rose and Snow played hide-and-seek in the grove of bearded giants, finally coming to rest on thrones of roots, wearing their forest crowns and eating their last berries in the speckled light.

"Snow!" Rose called, hopping down from her tangle of roots. She gestured for her sister to follow her.

"What is it?" Snow asked.

"I think it's smoke," Rose said.

Up from beds of curling ferns and mountain laurel, tendrils of smoke drifted out of the ground. The girls approached the smoke cautiously until they found its source.

"Is this a chimney?" Rose said, looking at a square, knee-high stack of carefully piled stones.

The girls circled the strange chimney, searching for more clues. Rose's shoe hit something solid hidden beneath leaves and weedy tendrils. She brushed away the forest floor, and they both knelt and peered at what Rose had uncovered.

It was a thick glass circle, framed in dark wood and set into the ground, with flowering moss growing around its edges. Snow tried to clean the film of hazy green from the glass. "Why is there a *window* in the ground?" Snow asked.

"Why is there a *chimney* in the ground?" Rose said. Then she looked up. "Snow, we're standing on somebody's—"

Snow put her nose right up to the glass, and her hair fell into the leaves. She looked up, finishing Rose's thought. "Somebody's *house*," she whispered.

Rose put her face to the window, too, but they couldn't see a thing. Rose stood up to look at the ground around them and saw something the color of brass glinting beneath the leaves. She pushed away the moss and uncovered a square wooden door braced with curved brass hinges.

Rose stood. "An entire house, all below the ground . . . ," she said.

She trailed off because she'd finally noticed how dark it had grown. All around them, the forest had gone a deep blue.

"Rats, it's just so *dark* in there," Snow said, without looking up from the window.

"It's so dark *out here*," Rose said, tugging Snow's arm.

"Hold on!" Snow said. She put her ear to the glass. "I can hear something. It's really quiet, but I think it's music." She looked up at Rose. "There's *music* coming from the ground!"

"Come on," Rose said impatiently. She couldn't hear anything, and she was too worried to listen. She pulled at the neck of Snow's dress as if it were a kitten's scruff. "We need to go home while we can still see the way."

Rose had a sense of where things were, maybe not enough to point north and south and east and west, but enough to guess what way was forward and what way was back. She looked through the grove of bearded trees. She imagined a little map in her head, then nodded to herself and turned back to Snow.

"I think it's this way." As Rose spoke, her voice fell.

For when Snow stood and brushed leaves from her dress, a pair of glowing eyes appeared in the distance, sparking in the darkening air. Then another. Then another.

CHAPTER 3
Wolves!

Rose stood stock-still in fading twilight. The yellow eyes barely blinked; the dark shapes that held them stood in an ominous huddle.

The wolves didn't move.

The girls didn't move.

"Crumbs," Snow said.

Rose's voice was just shy of a whimper. "Be . . . still," she breathed, trying with all her might not to sound afraid. "And they will go away."

"They don't seem like they are going away," Snow whispered. She grabbed a large branch and held it in front of them.

The wolves watched them, waiting for a silent signal, shifting from paw to paw beneath the bright moon hidden in the treetops.

"Get out of here," Snow shouted, waving her branch wildly. "Go!"

Then a huge wolf, twice as big as the others, emerged. It took its place at the front of the pack.

Snow lunged forward with her branch, wielding it like a sword. *"Go away!"*

Rose closed her eyes. "We're going to have to run." She grabbed Snow's hand and squeezed it hard.

The wolves looked to their big leader for permission, ready to spring forward.

"Ow!" Snow whispered, pulling her hand away. Then she looked at Rose's face and took her hand again, squeezing it back.

"If they catch up, we'll climb a tree," Rose said. She breathed in, trying to fill her chest with courage that wasn't there.

"One," Snow whispered. "Two. Three!"

Snow threw the branch down, and the girls turned and ran.

They tore through the ferns, cracking fallen branches, kicking up a wake of leaves. Snow and Rose raced through the grove of old trees, their gnarled trunks blurring on either side. Rose looked back over her shoulder.

A wolf howled.

"They're catching up," Rose said, stumbling to a stop. She grabbed at the sprawling roots of the closest tree and turned to Snow, gesturing wildly. "Climb!"

They scrabbled up the roots, and Rose swung herself onto the lowest branch. Below her, Snow's fingers slipped. Rose reached down and offered her hand.

The wolves were almost there. Snow could hear them breathing as she grabbed Rose's wrist and struggled to pull herself up.

Snow felt sharp teeth latch onto her shoe, tugging. She kicked as hard as she could, her pale legs dangling just a few feet off the ground. Rose pulled as hard as she thought she could, and then she pulled harder.

Snow's shoe came off, and the wolf jerked backward with its empty prize. Snow finally swung up on the crooked bend of the branch to sit with Rose.

Just then, a horn sounded.

The girls craned their necks to see where the sound had come from. The wolves turned and perked up their ears.

A hundred yards off, a silhouette appeared high on a bank. It flew down toward the clearing. The wolves shifted their attention between the girls in the tree and the approaching figure. As it drew closer, the shadow took the form of a tall man clothed in furs.

In his broad arm was a bow. He pulled an arrow from his hip.

"No!" Snow called out in a little yelp.

The wolves circled, confused and restless.

The Huntsman pulled his arm back, and Snow called out again. "No! Please don't!"

He paused, then loosed his arrow. The giant wolf howled in pain.

The wolves scattered. The Huntsman blew his horn again. It bellowed through the grove.

The girls jumped from the tree. Snow grabbed her abandoned shoe and pulled it on as she stumbled forward. They turned back, but the Huntsman was gone.

They ran through the dark, Rose's instincts leading her. It was easy, easier than she had imagined, as if the branches of the trees, the moss paths, the forest itself, led them back. Snow and Rose ran inside the little stone-and-wood cottage and locked the door behind them.

Their mother hadn't even wondered where they were.

X X X

That night, safe in their beds, Snow whispered to Rose, "I want to go back."

Rose opened her eyes. "Into the woods?"

"Yes," Snow answered.

"To the Underground House?" Rose asked.

"Of course!" Snow whisper-shouted.

Rose paused, looking up into the dark, silent air. Curiosity and fear bumped together in her chest like butterflies. "Me too," she said finally. "In the daytime. In the sunlight."

They made rules and plans for the woods that night.

One: they would go in daylight and be home by nightfall.

Two: they would go to the Underground House and find out who lived there.

And three: they wouldn't tell their mother about the wolves. They wouldn't tell her about anything that would make her worry.

After that was decided, they were silent for a few minutes before Snow's voice came again. "Rose?" she whispered.

"Mmm-hmm," Rose mumbled back.

"I keep thinking about that wolf." Her voice trembled. "The Huntsman shot it because of us. It might have died . . ." She trailed off. "Because of *us*."

"But what would we have done if he hadn't come?" Rose said.

"I don't know." Snow sighed. "It's still sad."

"I know," Rose said. But if it was a choice between them and the wolves, she would always choose herself and her sister. "I guess you are . . . remember what Mama used to say? 'Wolf-hearted.'"

"And what were you?" Snow wondered sleepily. "Wait, I remember." She yawned. "Good night, Rose the rabbit-hearted."

"Good night," Rose whispered back. Then she pulled the quilt tight around her and dreamed of wolves and thorns and arrows and the mysteries that live in the heart of the forest.

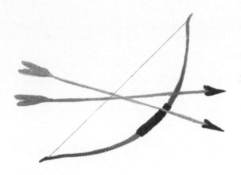

CHAPTER 4
A Curious Library

For days after that, Snow and Rose tried to find the Underground House. They would dart off the path, the way they had run before, past the stream and the grove of trees with their lichen beards, to the place they remembered finding the window in the ground, the chimney piled with stones. But there was nothing there, not even a wisp of smoke.

Either they were trying to find it in the wrong place, or the house didn't want to be found. After days of careful searching, of being home by sunset, Snow and Rose started wondering what lay on the *other* side of the path, to the east. They found something else, not hidden away but just as interesting. It stood in a bright clearing: a small, narrow house. The high walls and scalloped roof were made of wood, with an animal pen to one side. A lace carpet of white flowers grew ankle-high around it all.

There was a sign out front, the words COME IN painted in an arch above a pointing hand. Below the hand swung a sign with the word LIBRARY in curling white letters. Rose's heart leapt. The thing she missed most was their own library. Snow and Rose exchanged glances before making their way up the winding stone path toward the house.

Snow knocked on the door, and it swung open on its own. Inside, the house smelled like wet wool. The sound of their hellos echoed in the doorway. After a pause, Snow and Rose were answered by a goat's bleating, then the sound of heavy, uneven footsteps.

"Well, hello! Daisy, who is it?" An old woman came forward, in catawampus steps caused by her wooden leg. She wore a long-sleeved dress and a sweater that was unseasonably heavy for the end of summer. She peered over her glasses, pushing away silver hair escaped from an untidy bun. "Visitors! Library patrons!" She held a baby goat with black fur in her arms. The goat began to chew on a lock of the woman's hair.

"Are you the Librarian?" Rose asked, her voice shy.

The Librarian nodded. "And who are you?" she asked.

Snow and Rose introduced themselves. Then the Librarian introduced them first to Daisy the goat, then to the library itself.

She led them through the front hallway into the center of the house. The girls looked around, their eyes drifting up a spiral staircase of wood and metal that spun to the ceiling, nearly filling the room. It seemed impossibly high, as high as any treetops. "Please make yourselves at home," the Librarian said, placing the goat on the ground. The girls followed her as she made her way forward, the goat's hooves *clip-clopping* behind.

"You start here," the Librarian said, gesturing to the stairs.

The girls climbed the first few steps. Snow elbowed Rose, raising her eyebrow, and Rose shrugged. The sisters looked around, trying to understand what they saw. The Librarian didn't follow but called out after them. "Take all the time you need," she said. "I'll be in my office."

On every side of the staircase were intricate shelves built into the walls an arm's reach away. As the girls made their way up, they were further puzzled, for in this library, there weren't any books.

Instead, arranged on the shelves, nestled in nooks, displayed in boxes, stuffed into glass bottles, were hundreds—maybe thousands—of little objects. The girls became lost to the world, aware only of this enormous cabinet of curiosities. They climbed the steps silently, drifting up and apart, examining the contents of the shelves, each in her own dream.

The items were labeled in the same curling writing they'd seen on the sign out front, only instead of white paint, these were written in ink and smudged pencil. A bit of coral, a spotted feather, a scrap of velvet, a paper crane, a delicate bone, a pebble of fool's gold, a ball of twine, a wooden spool, a slip of soap, a scrap of brown paper, a lock of hair, a scallop shell, a crooked spoon, a postage stamp, an acorn, a baby tooth, a silver button.

Rose took in a sharp breath as her eye caught an object on a shelf near her shoulder. She grabbed a bit of golden chain, thinking of her father's watch. It slid into her hand like a little snake, not a memory come to life, just a bracelet with a broken clasp.

Snow cleared her throat and called down through the bars of the staircase. "I don't mean to be rude . . ." She looked at the silver bun below and called out to its owner. "But I thought this was a library?"

The Librarian had settled at an unruly desk that lay tucked below, off to the side of the main room. "My dear, this *is* a library."

Rose climbed to where Snow stood peering at something beneath a tiny magnifying glass. Snow looked at Rose through the magnifying glass; Rose eyed her back with a warning glance.

"What she means," Rose said, "is do you have any . . . *books*?"

"Cookies?" the Librarian called up to them.

"Books," Rose tried again as the girls reluctantly came down the stairs.

"Yes, I heard you. Fancy some cookies, though?" the Librarian asked. "Mostly just bits, but probably a few wholes." They could see her busying herself with clinking plates while a new goat, a bigger one with white fur, munched on scattered paper.

Snow and Rose joined her at her desk, settling down awkwardly in two rickety chairs. The Librarian retrieved a battered tin from her desk drawer and dumped a heap of crumbs onto a chipped plate.

"What is a library made of?" she said in that way people do when they know they've asked a tricky question. She offered the plate to the girls.

"A whole lot of books," Snow answered, thinking of

their old library and its tall sliding ladders. The black baby goat clopped up to the desk and began to chew one of Rose's braids.

The Librarian shook her head. "Wrong." She took a bite of cookie. "A whole lot of *stories*."

The girls looked up at all those shelves holding all those little things. Rose pulled her braid away from the goat.

"I've got stories to last you the rest of your days," the Librarian said. "Lovely ones, strange ones, comedies, tragedies. The shelves are full of all those things."

The girls looked skeptical.

"If you don't believe me, check something out," the Librarian said, waving her hand high in the air. "If you don't like it, simply return it." Then she murmured to herself, "But they'll be needing cards." She rifled through the piles on her desk and muttered a reminder to herself: "Library cards, goose." She rummaged in her desk and produced another dented tin. "Oh yes. Here we go."

The old woman drew out two cards, like ordinary playing cards but with pictures in place of the suits. "How old are you?" she asked, shuffling the cards as she looked at Snow.

"Nine," Snow said. "Almost ten."

"So there's a nine for you . . . ," the woman said. She presented a card with nine yellow stars to Snow.

"And you?" the Librarian asked, thumbing through the worn deck.

"Eleven," Rose answered.

"Rats. Are you sure you're not ten?" she asked. "Well, this'll do." The Librarian gave Rose a card with a number one printed in the four corners, and a picture of a single ship in the center.

"Now you must find something to check out!" the Librarian said, smiling. "One story each."

Snow and Rose returned to the staircase and slowly made their way back up through the shelves. They weren't sure how they were supposed to *know*.

As if she heard their thoughts, the Librarian called up to them, "Don't worry, something will choose *you*."

After another turn up and down the stairs, as the afternoon sun began to flare in the windows, the girls made their selections. Rose picked a small pair of scissors. Snow chose a little brass key.

They presented their items to the Librarian, who took their cards and made an indecipherable mark on each before handing them back.

"How long can we keep them?" Rose asked.

"How long is a piece of string?" the Librarian said,

then ushered the girls to the door. They waved good-bye, and the goats bleated.

As the sisters walked home, the objects tucked in their pockets, Rose joked to Snow, "Mine isn't telling me a story yet."

"Maybe it will later," Snow said. "Maybe it just takes a little while."

"Do you want to go back soon?" Rose asked, not sure herself what to think of the library or the Librarian.

"We have to wait for our stories," Snow said, bumping Rose's shoulder.

When Snow and Rose returned to the cottage, they told their mother what they'd found. She looked at them as if through a fog. Then she nodded in a way that made them unsure if she actually believed or had even heard them.

Snow went off to find Earl Grey, and Rose went to their little bookshelf—all that remained of their old library, the real kind of library, not one made of scissors and keys and baby goats. She pulled out a book bound in dark blue leather that was so big it took both arms to hold it open. Rose curled up, turning through beautiful maps of faraway places until she found the part she loved best, called "The Seven Wonders."

Their father had to travel far and wide, but no matter where he went, he never liked to be away from home for long. He read to Snow and Rose about the Seven Wonders, and he would say, "But there are three wonders better than any in the world," before he kissed the girls on their heads.

Rose pulled out the card the Librarian had given her, with the picture of the ship. She thought back to the night she had asked her father when they would see the Seven Wonders together. As Rose traced her fingers over the pages now, she remembered how her heart had sunk when her father told her that most of them weren't there anymore.

She also remembered what he'd said just afterward, seeing her disappointment. "Oh, Rosie, there are still wonders left in the world."

Rose closed the heavy book in her lap. As she stood to go help her mother start dinner, Rose felt a sharp jab at her side: the scissors. It reminded her of the Librarian and all those objects on all those shelves. She wondered if the library qualified as a wonder, a modest kind of wonder, but still. Her father would have liked it.

As Rose walked to the kitchen, she thought of her father's things, wondering where they were now, this moment. She listed them to herself in silence: *a watch . . . a blanket . . . a knife . . .*

X X X

The knife was still in the forest, and the ivory handle grew warm as someone turned it over in his hands, admiring it, his finger tracing the bird's feathers. The blade caught his reflection as he closed it gently and hid it away.

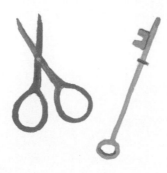

CHAPTER 5

The Mushroom Boy

S now and Rose tried to find their way back to the Underground House again, but they grew tired of looking. They listened for the music with their ears close to the ground, but there was only the quiet chirp and rustle of the forest. They sifted through leaves, staining their dresses with moss, but couldn't find a trace of a windowpane or hinge.

Snow drifted back to the hillside, back to watch the old house. They started to return to their routines from the first weeks in the cottage. The only difference was that once or twice Rose saw Snow fish out the key from the library and look at it, waiting for it to do something.

But soon there was a new nip in the air, and everything began to look different as the beginning of
autumn set in. One morning, after a breakfast of warm
oats and milk, their mother disappeared into her room
and reappeared with two bundles. Snow's bundle was a
cardigan the color of a sparrow's egg. Rose's was a pull-
over stitched from yarn the color of red winterberries.

Wrapped in their new sweaters, Snow and Rose felt
inspired to go off in search of the Underground House
one more time. The woods were sun-dappled as the
girls hopped over the stream. On the other side, a frog
two sizes too big stared out at them with eyes like black
marbles. Snow and Rose looked at each other, then hurried past the old-man grove and on to the clearing.

Today, the sisters covered different patches, walking
carefully, feeling for hidden clues beneath their feet for
what felt like the hundredth time.

They found nothing. They traced their steps the
way the wolves had chased them, circled back to the
stream, and followed the water. "Maybe it was *never*
there," Rose said. She pulled her sweater sleeves down
over her thumbs to warm her hands. "Maybe—"

Snow stopped suddenly. "Wait!" she called out. She
held her finger to her lips and looked at Rose. They
had come to a new place, where the woods were deeply
shadowed.

Snow and Rose waded into a sea of ferns so dense they couldn't see their feet below. "Maidenhair and staghorn and—" Rose recited quietly to herself, making notes as the ferns brushed her legs.

"Shhh!" Snow hushed her. "I hear it!"

Rose strained her ears. "I don't hear anything."

Snow led her farther through the ferns that swayed above their knees.

Rose could hear the music now, faint in the crisp, chilly air.

"Look for a door in the ground," Rose reminded Snow, though she needed no reminding. They followed the music to a tree. It was circled in roots that curled in and out of the ground in arches big enough to crawl through.

All of a sudden, the music seemed much closer.

Snow went down on her hands and knees to crawl into the roots, until only the bottom halves of her legs were above the ground. Then she scooted backward and looked up, her face smudged with dirt.

"This is it!" Snow said, jittery with excitement. "There's a tunnel under this tree."

Rose's fingers started to worry. She looked at Snow.

"I'll go first," Snow said. In a blink, she dove back in. Rose heard her muffled voice—"Are you behind me?"— before the last of Snow's boot vanished from sight.

Rose breathed in. She worried about what was beyond the tunnel. Then she had to stop thinking, because Snow was gone. "Yes," Rose called back, and crawled in after her.

The tunnel was dark and winding: a small labyrinth under the tree, knotted and bumped, hung overhead with tendrils. A blue-green glow came up through the root walls as they followed the music, crawling down through a thousand years of growing.

Suddenly, there was a steep drop where the tunnel gave way to nothing. Snow slid forward, and Rose tumbled after her. They landed with two bumps.

"Crumbs," Snow muttered. She looked up, blinking slowly. Rose grabbed her satchel and rubbed her sore knees. She looked around, trying to get her bearings.

The music had stopped. They were in a cavern, an underground room. The walls glowed faintly in the blue-green light, and all around them was the smell of earth.

A warm yellow light appeared from around a bend. A lantern came into view, just before the person carrying it.

"Who are you, then?" the boy asked. His voice was gentle and lifted up at the end.

The boy's face was pale, with dark eyes and a snarl of brown hair. The rest of him was spindly. It was hard to tell how old he was: he was about as tall as Rose, but skinnier than either of the sisters. He wore a moth-eaten sweater that might've once been white and a pair of patched brown trousers. The beginning of a smile played at the corners of his mouth.

The girls stood and brushed themselves off.

"Who are you?" Rose said, fixing her hair and brushing leaves from Snow's back.

The boy laughed, one of those half-finished laughs that barely escape, as Snow untangled a length of root from her hair.

Snow shot him a look. "Yes, who are *you?*"

"Ibo," he said. The boy took a handkerchief from his pocket and blew his nose.

"Bebo?" Snow said, laughing.

His cheeks grew rosy in the lantern light. "Ivo, I said. I-V-O." The boy shifted his feet. "Anyway, you're the ones who tumbled into my farm. What are your names?"

"I'm Rose, and she's Snow." Rose hoped she sounded friendly enough to make up for Snow. "Um . . . how do you do?"

"People who've got strange names shouldn't throw stones," Ivo said, shooting a look at Snow. He fidgeted, and both girls noticed that, instead of gloves, he wore on his hands a pair of old woolen socks, cut off at the toes. "You don't look like you're from here, then," he

added, glancing at the delicate embroidery stitched into the hems of their dresses.

"Well, that's because we're not," Snow replied.

Rose wondered if that was still true, after all this time in the woods.

"And how'd you get to the farm?" the boy asked.

"We sort of fell," Rose said. Ivo smiled. "We crawled into the tunnel because we heard music."

"Do you know who plays it?" Snow asked. Her voice took on a different, excited tone.

"I do," Ivo said, looking pleased.

The girls explained how they'd first found the chimney at the beginning of summer, how they'd been looking ever since.

Ivo's eyes lit up. "That was the two of you, then? Pawing around the front door?" He laughed. "Oh, Mum was so worried. She hid us well after that." The boy looked at them with serious eyes. "There are dangerous things, things that shouldn't be . . ." His voice trailed off.

"Well, we're very dangerous," Rose joked nervously, then saw that he didn't smile. "What *things* do you mean?"

"Yes, what kinds of things?" Snow repeated.

"Well, the big creatures, mostly. The Menace of the Woods, we call it," Ivo replied.

Rose's eyebrows knitted together. She looked

sideways at Snow. She thought of the blackbird and the big wolf and the frog.

"And there are other things, things you can't see, but you just get a feeling sometimes. . . ." Ivo stopped when he saw the girl's expressions. "I didn't mean to scare you," he said. "Just—be careful, that's all."

"What is this place, anyway?" Snow asked.

Ivo smiled. "I'll show you." He led with his lantern, and they followed him through one, two, three bends in the cavern.

"Here we are, then," said Ivo.

There was a faint musty smell. In some places it was like barely moldy bread; in other places, like a sweater packed away in a chest and unfolded a year later. The walls were dimly lit with the same glow the sisters had seen before, and Ivo held his lantern in the center of the room, casting more light onto its contents. There were mushrooms everywhere. Tiny ones grew alongside giants, their caps glowing scarlet and pink, biscuity brown, and ghostly white in the dark of the cavern. They grew round, squat, branching, and slender. Each kind grew neatly on its own carpet of moss, rising out of the earth.

Rose put her hand to a stretch of glowing wall and looked at Ivo quizzically.

"Lantern moss. Otherwise we'd only have these,"

Ivo said, swinging his lantern. "A few of the mushrooms glow a bit, like those near your head, Snow. Starlights, we call them."

Snow turned and saw a patch of delicate white mushrooms. They seemed to reach out to her. She stretched her index finger to touch one, and when she pulled it back, the faintest luminescent dust was traced on her fingertip.

"But it's not enough for proper light," Ivo added.

"So what are all these mushrooms for?" Snow asked.

"All sorts of things," Ivo replied. "Some are just for ordinary eating, some for medicine. A few, I don't want to *know* who buys them."

Rose gazed at the dark garden around her. "Do you know all their names?" she asked, her face lit with lantern moss.

"Well, I don't know their proper names," he said a bit sheepishly. "Only what we call them."

Rose nodded. "So what about these?" She pointed to a blush variety.

"Dancer's Skirts," said Ivo.

"And these?"

Ivo and Snow came to her side, and as Rose pointed, the boy recited: "Milliner's Thimbles, Ruby Toadstools, Flea's Parasols, Moon Giants, Golden Pence, Butterscotch Tinies, Devil's Buttons, Mouse's

Buttons. Come to think of it, there's a lot with *buttons* in the name."

Rose clapped her hands in appreciation. "But why is this so far from your house?"

"Well, the earth there isn't exactly right for growing," Ivo replied.

"But don't you ever get scared down here by yourself?" Rose asked.

"I don't mind it," Ivo said. He smiled his crooked smile. "I was born in the dark."

"What about the music?" Snow said impatiently, then added a late attempt at politeness. "Not to interrupt . . ."

Ivo's eyes lit up, and he disappeared into the tunnels. While they waited, Rose stood on her tiptoes to see what grew on the highest shelves. Snow sniffed a patch of lantern moss and sneezed.

When Ivo returned, he was cradling a violin in his arms. He produced a thin bow and sat on one of the stumps scattered through the cavern for seating. Then he proceeded to play. It was the same mysterious music they'd heard in the warm summer twilight at the Underground House, and then again today.

"That's it!" Snow said, beaming. "I play the violin, too."

Ivo held his bow silent in midair. "This is a fiddle," he said, his voice confident.

"I'm pretty sure it's a *violin*," Snow corrected.

"Fiddle," Ivo said.

"Violin."

Rose loudly cleared her throat. "We should probably be going soon." She turned to Ivo. "How do we get back up outside? If the way down is, well, *falling down*."

"Don't you know how to fall up?" he said. "No, I'm only fooling. Don't worry, there's stairs." He placed his fiddle carefully on the stump and showed them the secret way back aboveground and into the sunlight.

"Before you go, can I show you something else?" he asked.

Both Snow and Rose nodded.

Ivo's "something else" was a single mushroom, round and deep blue, like a dark pearl made of paper. It filled Ivo's palm as he displayed it to each of the girls in turn.

"I've been waiting to show this to somebody for ages," he said. "It's called Sandman's Pocket. I discovered it. I named it, too," he said proudly.

"What does it do?" Snow said, peering down at it.

"You'll see," he said. He scanned the ferns and the mossed tree trunks around them. "There!" He pointed to a pair of squirrels skittering a few yards away. Ivo tossed the mushroom. There was a great puff of shimmering blue smoke as it landed, breaking apart between the two squirrels.

"I forgot to say," Ivo added, holding his nose, "it's probably best if you don't breathe in."

The girls held their breath.

The squirrels froze in mid-skitter, then appeared to drop dead.

"Oh, you *wicked* boy!" Snow cried.

"No, they're just asleep!" Rose exclaimed. "You said 'Sandman's something,' right? So they're only sleeping. Aren't they?"

Ivo looked terrified.

"*Aren't* they?" Rose demanded.

The squirrels lay on the ground, not moving so much as a whisker.

"Of course!" Ivo said, bewildered. "They'll wake up. It just takes a while to wear off." His cheeks flushed with the realization that maybe this hadn't been his best idea. "It's just a bit of fun. They'll wake up good as new," he reassured Snow. He looked at the ground. "I should have warned you."

The girls stood over the squirrels as Ivo waited. After a few more silent minutes, the squirrels began to twitch back to life. Then they scampered up a tree and out of sight.

"So you're not a squirrel murderer," Snow said, still scowling.

"Just a squirrel Sandman," Ivo said.

"We've never known many boys," Rose said. "We didn't know if that was, I don't know, something you'd do for fun."

"I guess I've never made friends with any girls." He looked at the sisters. "There aren't that many friends to make here, really."

Ivo pulled his sleeves down over his sock-gloved fingers, as Rose had done earlier. Around them the nip in the air was growing sharper, sending them back to their homes, above and under the ground. They traded awkward goodbyes, and the girls started back toward the cottage but turned when they heard Ivo call out, "Hey!"

He added, "Maybe you'll come back sometime?" His voice sounded hopeful.

He couldn't see their faces, but Rose smiled, and Snow did, too.

"Maybe so," Snow called back.

At dinnertime that night, their mother, who didn't hear many reports from their wanderings, heard all about the mysterious music that had led them to a cavern underground. Snow and Rose told her about mushrooms called Mouse's Buttons and Dancer's Skirts, and about their new friend, Ivo, who'd been born in the dark and played the fiddle underground.

CHAPTER 6
Provisions

Twice a year, when the day is half-dark and half-light, in a town a day's journey away, the Equinox Market came. Merchants arrived from near and far, selling fruit and animals and tools and perfume and cloth and spices. In Snow and Rose's old life, it was a place the servants had gone. Now, for the first time, their mother went on her own, leaving Snow and Rose to take care of each other.

Their mother's wagon was drawn by a black bicycle. The cart was a present from their old gardener—in its past life, it had carried shrubs and gardener's tools. When their mother returned from the Equinox

Market, the cart was filled with glass jars, clinking against crates that held bunches of herbs and bushels of vegetables and fruit. On top of it all, securely bound, was a wire cage.

Inside the cage was a beautiful chicken that had golden-brown feathers and laid speckled brown eggs. Snow immediately took her from the cage and held her, even as the round little bird squawked and flapped her wings to get free. Their mother told Snow and Rose that when she was small, she'd had a brown-feathered chicken she loved, and that her name was Goldie.

"Let's name our chicken Goldie, too," Snow said.

"Would that make her Goldie Junior?" Rose asked.

"Goldie the Second," Snow said, nodding in approval.

Their mother looked pleased with the provisions she'd brought back. She seemed capable, as though the heaviness around her had lightened. She tied on an apron and the scarf she used to wear in her sculptor's studio to keep dust out of her hair. She showed Snow and Rose how to make a chicken pen inside the tin shed. Back in the house, their mother gathered pots and laid out cutting boards and knives to make food to store for the cold season that would come.

"I saw your friend at the market, the young mushroom farmer," their mother said, handing each of the girls an apron. "He was helping his parents."

"Ivo?" Snow asked, tying her apron.

"So that's where he was!" Rose said. "We went to his farm. I wondered if we were looking in the wrong place again." She smoothed her apron and straightened the bow, then dug into a sack, retrieving bundles and packets.

"We have to prepare," their mother said. She tucked a stray lock of dark hair beneath her scarf.

"Prepare for what?" Snow mumbled, her mouth full of peach.

"For winter," their mother answered. "Luckily, I remember how. We had to make things for ourselves when I was little." She smiled, a small smile, but rare and reassuring. She scooted the bushel of peaches away from Snow. "For when I can't just make my way down the path to the village, and it's too cold for anything to grow. So don't eat everything now."

Snow eyed the crates of empty jars. "We're going to fill all of these?" she asked, frowning. "But we just made Goldie's house."

"So we'll have eggs," her mother replied. "But won't you want anything else to eat when the snow comes?"

Snow wiped peach juice from her cheek. She looked at her mother skeptically and nodded.

"Then you need to learn to cook." Her mother held out a wooden spoon.

Snow eyed the spoon. "We should have someone to cook *for* us."

"Oh no," Rose said quietly, busying herself at the sink with a bowl of red currants.

"We're *all* going to be cooks now," her mother said, cutting a melon in half with a sharp chop. "It will be fun."

"But I don't want to be a cook!" Snow said, panic growing in her voice. She untied her apron and threw it on the floor. She could hear a clamor starting in her ears, the sound before a symphony, of stray horns and disordered strings.

Her mother sighed. "Learning to feed yourself doesn't mean you'll grow up to be a cook."

"I'm not doing it," Snow said.

Her mother's voice was calm but serious. "Since we have come here, I've been doing almost everything myself. And now I am just asking for a little bit of help." She touched Snow's cheek. "We are all we've got."

Snow laced up her boots, scowling the whole time.

"I'm going to look for somewhere else to live." In her ears, the clamor began to grow louder and louder.

"And what will you eat when it's cold?" her mother asked.

"I guess I'll just starve!" Snow shouted, closing the door hard behind her.

X X X

Snow sat in her favorite part of the Snow Garden, her garden, back in her old life. Earl Grey had followed her on the long walk out of the woods, down the hill, into the valley. He sat beside her as she breathed in a wall of white blooms until her anger grew quiet enough for her to think. She wondered how people got to be the way they were. Why things angered her so, why they ran away with her, when they didn't bother Rose.

Their mother said Snow had their father's temper, but Snow could only remember his anger running away with him once. It was several years ago. Four big horses had thundered up the drive, and their coachman hadn't noticed the two small girls, and the wheels barely missed them. Their father's face was usually kind, but it became red and furious. He pulled the man down from his seat and held him by the collar of his shirt, upbraiding him for his carelessness. She knew he was this way because they'd been in danger, but the person he was in that moment—she almost didn't know him.

Snow had forgotten about her anger some days in the woods. The day they found the library. The day they found Ivo. But today she remembered it, or it remembered her. When she thought she had outrun it, it always seemed to find her.

Snow thought of Rose, happy and patient in the kitchen at the old house. Now Rose made them dinner at the cottage sometimes, when her mother wasn't up to it or when she'd gone to the market. Snow didn't know how to make much more than slightly burned toast.

As she watched the white swan gliding slowly on the surface of the pond, Snow made a wish in the garden that she could be patient. That she wouldn't let her anger run away with her. Snow stayed among the last of the year's white flowers until the shadows got long.

Then quietly, with Earl Grey at her side, she crept up to the house. She saw herself barely reflected in the window. Inside, the dining room was framed perfectly, a moving picture, bright against the darkening blue outside. People she didn't know, a mother and a father and three children, were sitting at the dining table, her dining table. The servants brought out a big roasted turkey.

"*My* turkey," she said, looking down at Earl Grey. "Of course, I would share with you."

"What's that?" A warm, creaking voice came from somewhere behind Snow.

She turned and saw Marcel, the old gardener, wearing the same big green coat he always wore. The look on his face split the uneasy difference between a smile and a frown.

"You know you shouldn't be here, love."

Snow looked down, her cheeks growing hot.

"I told you, you can come to the gardens anytime. Anytime. But you can't be creeping around the house, no—no, that you can't do." The gardener's crepe-papery eyes crinkled, and the stubbly shadow of his mustache curved into another sad smile.

X X X

When Snow returned to the cottage, she was amazed to find that her mother and Rose had hung the top of the pantry with upside-down bouquets of rosemary and garlic grass and sage. They'd filled all the jars with red currant preserves and peaches and plum tomatoes, big chunks of melon and squash. Pots bubbled on the stove. The house smelled like blackberry jam.

Snow stood and looked silently, first at her mother, then at Rose. "Is there anything that I can do?"

"You can stir the jam," her mother said, handing Snow the spoon again, as if she didn't remember the tantrum, as if Snow had never left.

CHAPTER 7
The Little Man

O n a windy fall morning, Ivo took Snow and Rose foraging for mushrooms growing wild. He knew which ones were good to eat and which were full of poison, and he taught the girls to tell the difference. In dark nooks and the shade of fallen trees, they found two different kinds to fill up their baskets: a cream-yellow kind that looked almost like a blossom, and a short, plump kind that Ivo called a Penny Bun. Now that they could find him, they went to Ivo's tree to look for him. Now that they knew him, if too many days passed, they started to miss him.

Their next stop was an orchard of crab apple trees, where the wild October air rustled the leaves and made the fruit sway in heavy red bunches. The girls filled their baskets and helped Ivo finish filling his own cloth sack.

Ivo tossed a tiny apple into his mouth, crunching it. "They'll be expecting me back home before the afternoon's all the way gone." He slung the bag of apples over his shoulder with his other foraged bundles.

The girls frowned.

"They're worriers, Papa and Mum," Ivo said, shrugging. "If they had their way, I'd only ever be at the farm or at home. They don't like me to go too far by myself."

"But you're not by yourself," Rose said.

"You know what I mean." Ivo waved goodbye, and the sisters gathered their baskets. They waved back, and Ivo turned homeward.

Rose and Snow were about to start home themselves, when they heard a rustling from behind the trees. A big brown hare, much larger than the bunnies they'd seen in summer, came darting out of the undergrowth and dashed away. The wind blew through the trees, making a hushing sound in the dry leaves, and the woods around them shivered.

Then came a great crash, shaking the leaves like

a sudden hurricane. Snow and Rose heard the sound of thrashing wings and breaking branches, and then a high, whining shriek.

The girls followed the sound to the other side of the apple trees. There, the huge blackbird they'd seen in early summer was high up in a tall oak tree, holding something in its claws. Rose knew it was the same bird, because she caught a flash of the white mark on its chest.

"Maybe that bird *was* trying to get you," said Snow, her eyes wide.

Rose looked up, trying to catch a glimpse of the battle. "It looks like a person, sort of. But it's too small." She gasped. "Is it a baby?"

"I think it has a beard!" Snow said, peering up.

"Whoever he is," Rose said, "the bird is going to shake him to death." As the little someone dangled overhead, he noticed the girls below.

"Hellllllllllllllllpppp!" he howled, flailing. The bird thrashed, and his little body flew, a wisp of cream-colored beard trailing through the air.

The girls looked at each other, hoping the other had an idea. Now they could barely hear the Little Man grumbling above the clamor. They only made out a hiss: "You deserve worse, you fool."

"What?" Snow called.

"Lovely girls, don't just stand there!" he howled down at them. The bird squawked loudly then, dangling him from the back of his little brown coat. The blackbird seemed to eye the sisters as he swung the Little Man, thudding, into the tree trunk.

"It's not polite to just"—he hit the tree with a violent *thunk*—"go on *staring*!"

Rose was too wary of the bird to climb the tree, but she had an idea. She tossed a handful of apples into the air, and the enormous bird opened its beak to snap them up, freeing the Little Man.

"Oh, clever girl!" he cried. But the instant the Little Man caught himself on a branch, the bird dove and snatched him in its claws. The bird perched, holding its captive dangling over the girls' heads.

Snow jumped into the air, grabbing hold of the Little Man's leg.

"I shall be ripped to shreds," he sobbed.

Rose grabbed onto the other tiny leg, and now they were in a tug-of-war with the blackbird.

"I'm being rescued by waifs," the Little Man shrieked, his beard billowing up in a huff.

"It's not very *polite* to insult your rescuers!" Rose shouted.

"They might *let go*, you ungrateful—" Snow said, giving his leg a fierce tug.

At this last tug, there was ripping sound as the Little Man's coat finally gave way, leaving a scrap of wool in the bird's claws.

The Little Man landed in a bush, and the bird flew furiously up and out of sight. The scrap of wool coat fluttered to the ground.

The girls ran to the small bearded heap.

"Who are you?" Rose asked.

"*What* are you?" Snow interrupted.

He pulled himself up to his full height, reaching just under Snow's nose. "*That* is not a very polite question to ask someone about himself, girl, so I will answer the other." He combed the leaves from his wispy cream-colored beard, which glinted in the light with a faint cast of gold.

"I have been called many names over many years," he said, smoothing his beard. He was suddenly possessed of a strange calm. The girls exchanged glances, confused about how quickly he seemed to have recovered from his terror.

The Little Man examined the tear in his coat and continued. "Sometimes I'm the Dwarf and sometimes I'm the Tomten. . . ." He paused and produced, seemingly from nowhere, a spool of thread.

"Or sometimes the Brownie or Boggart or Gnome,"

he said, spinning once around. When he stopped, his clothes were mended and tidy again.

"And to some very rude people, I've been the Goblin." He looked at the girls, and his eyes flashed for an instant in the bright daytime forest, the way a cat's eyes sometimes do in the dark.

"But these are just names," he said.

He crouched and began sifting through a pile of leaves. After a moment, he retrieved a leather hat the color of deerskin. He placed it on his head and straightened himself. "I know every bramble and branch of this forest. I know every creature, every bee and mouse and fox. I know when arrows fall, and I know what the trees saw. I know things nobody knows." He faced the girls, and his eyes flashed again. "Many names have I, child. But none have guessed *what* I am."

Rose felt the hairs on the back of her neck prickle.

"And what, pray tell, are your names?" he asked, setting his chin on his hand.

Snow looked at Rose, and they were both silent for a moment. When they answered, reluctantly, his eyes almost seemed to register recognition.

The Little Man smiled, saying, "Snow and Rose, such civilized girls. Now I must thank you properly."

He held his hands out at his sides as if offering something. "You may have an answer or a gift."

"Gift!" Snow cried out immediately, as if he'd offered a plate of something delicious and she was terribly hungry.

"Wait," Rose said. "What kind of an answer? To what kind of a question?"

"Well, the answer doesn't matter, because she's already chosen," the Little Man said.

"But we didn't know the rules," Rose said. She sensed something held just out of reach, like a catch at her back that wouldn't let her step forward. She had lost a chance to ask a question everyone around them had long since stopped asking.

"No finer thing than a gift, child!" the Little Man said. Something sharp in his voice made Rose go silent. He smiled at Snow. His smile curled up into his cheeks. "So! You must have your present, then. Close your eyes and hold out your right hand."

Snow shut her eyes tight, holding out her hand.

Rose kept her eyes open a sliver. She wasn't going to just stand there, trusting and blind, holding out her hands to someone who spoke in riddles and didn't have a name. Through the half-drawn curtains of her eyelids, Rose saw the Little Man gather leaves in his hands, then turn his back. Then she heard a sound like someone rummaging through pockets that never ended. His turned back made her bold, and she opened her eyes.

"Everywhere am I," the Little Man's voice scolded.

This startled Rose so much that she squeezed her eyes shut, and she didn't open them again until she felt something cool and smooth in her hand. Snow squealed beside her, and Rose saw that each of them held in their hands a beautiful miniature cake. The cakes were thickly frosted in pale violet icing and sat on dishes made of pressed sugar. The tops were studded with real violets, daintier and more lovely than anything the cooks had ever made for them.

"How did you make those?" Rose asked, her eyebrows knitted together.

"Oh, but that is my secret," the Little Man said.

"But you can't make something out of nothing," Rose pressed. Her eyes searched his face, his thin little hands.

"Again, I thank you," the Little Man said, removing his hat with a nod. "And now I must be gone."

Before Rose could stop her, Snow had bitten into her cake. Now she stood with a full mouth, looking around. "Where did he go?" Snow mumbled. Rose shook her head, baffled. She dropped her cake on the ground before Snow could ask for it.

Snow's stomach made a gurgling sound, and she looked at Rose like she might be sick. Snow coughed something into her hand, then uncurled her fingers, revealing not a sugared violet petal but a small brown leaf.

Rose looked around them but found nothing. The Little Man had vanished.

WHAT THE TREES KNEW

"I want him gone," the young one said. "He should be in the black earth, ground underfoot for the worms to feast."

"He will be someday," the old one said, in a calm voice, swaying the branches.

"How did he become?" the young one asked.

"He was once like us," the old one said. "But he went astray. Learn from his disgrace."

"It is happening," the young one said. A shower of dry leaves spun, dancing in the air.

"We will watch them," the old one said. "We will see."

CHAPTER 8
The Bear

Just before autumn faded, it burned bright with gusts of electric air, with the smell of wood smoke, everything dressed in gold and scarlet and bitter browns. This is when Snow's birthday came.

A week beforehand, the girls went to the village with their mother to get butter and flour and a spool of ribbon. Then the girls found beeswax for candles while their mother picked out a few surprise things.

Before they reached home, Snow and Rose asked to gather some branches of winterberry and some especially nice pinecones, and their mother went on ahead. Rose was worried as she chose the prettiest ones. She knew no matter how many pinecone garlands they made, the party would be more modest than the birthdays they used to have.

"Do you know my birthday wish?" Snow called.

"You're not supposed to tell," Rose answered.

Snow ignored her. "That it won't be long till everything goes back to the way it was."

Rose sighed. "But—"

"It can't hurt to wish," Snow said, busying herself with branches of white berries. "My other wish is that we will have some kind of really, really good cake." She paused. "With no leaves in it."

Rose laughed softly. "How is the fat Earl Grey?" she asked, steering the subject from birthday things. "I think he hides from me."

"Fat as ever. Fatter, actually," Snow said. "I didn't think it was possible."

Rose saw something barely catch in the light and wandered toward it. Strung from a low branch, just at eye level, was a beautiful spiderweb. She saw the spider, diligently unwinding her thread, swinging and fastening it in fragile angles. Rose watched the web growing before her eyes, thread by thread, until suddenly the web trembled.

She heard a strangled roar, low and desperate, howling through the trees. Rose turned from the spider and looked around for the source of the wild sound. It was something fiercer than the blackbird, bigger than the wolves. "Snow?" she called out.

The roar came again.

Rose called for Snow again. Then she walked quietly, following the sound, knotting and unknotting her fingers. In her bones, Rose knew the roar came from something hurt.

At the place the sound began, she found the bear.

He was enormous. Bigger than any bear Rose's mind would ever conjure when she'd ask it to picture a bear. His troubled presence filled the woods. His fur shone a brown so deep it was nearly black, glinting cinnamon in the places where sunlight fell on him.

The bear let out another bellow. He flung himself up so he stood, towering, on his great hind paws. He ripped at the tree beside him, leaving deep gashes in the gray bark.

"Snow?" Rose called again, her voice urgent.

The bear landed with all four feet back on the ground. He let out something like a sigh and swung his great head around. And the bear saw Rose.

She darted behind a tree, then peeked around it.

The bear looked at her, and she looked back. His eyes were dark and gentle, surprising things to find in such a fearsome head.

The bear struggled against something with his hind leg, but Rose couldn't make out what it was. She could tell, though, that he couldn't move. Slowly, carefully, she crept closer. When she was close enough to hear him breathe, close enough to touch his nose of black leather, she could see the blood on the leaves and the trap that held him.

Rose had never seen anything as cruel as this trap. It was as wide around as a tree trunk, with two rows of teeth that had snapped shut on the bear's leg, holding him captive.

The bear lowered his head, and Rose inched closer. Something about seeing such a fierce creature in such a pitiful state muffled the pounding of her rabbit heart and silenced the voice of caution in her ears. Rose thought of the fable about the mouse that saves the lion.

Then Snow's voice came from over her shoulder. "Poor thing." Her voice was soft, even as the bear thrashed. Snow came to stand beside Rose. "I can't believe you got so close to him," Snow said.

"We've got to do something," Rose said.

She looked at Snow, and together they approached the trap. They looked at the metal jaw, biting through fur and skin. Rose gently picked up the iron chain, and the reverberations made the bear flinch and growl.

"There are springs on either side of the teeth part,"

Rose said. She studied the trap, realizing what they had to do. "If we each press on one side, we might get it to open."

Rose trembled as they knelt at the bear's side.

"It might hurt him when we do," Snow said. Her face was filled with worry. "Maybe there's a less scary way?"

Rose tried to sound sure. "The only way is the scary way."

"Wait!" Snow said. She saw a small round hole in the metal. "The key!" Snow searched the pockets of her dress and held the key out triumphantly.

She placed it into the keyhole of the trap and turned. They heard the metal spring open.

The bear gave a terrible roar and shook his weight from side to side. The girls stumbled backward. But the girls weren't the only thing the bear shook free; the trap lay open on the forest floor.

The bear snorted. He looked at the girls once more and lowered his head in something like a bow or a nod. Then he thundered away through the trees, his magnificent size almost, but not quite, masking his limp.

"Things in the woods seem to need a lot of help," Snow said.

They heaved the trap into a hollow place in the

ground and kicked dirt over the top. "Do you need res-cuing? We are your girls!" Rose joked.

"We have experience helping everything, from little people to giant bears," Snow said in her best salesman's voice. Then she added, "I think Papa would be proud."

Each time he'd gone away, their father had made them promise: "You must be helpful and you must be brave." He had meant helpful to their mother, to the servants. To be brave in ordinary ways, like hurt knees or bad dreams. Now the sisters' eyes, dark green and pale blue, looked at each other, sad and proud at the same time. "We didn't get a lot of chances before," Rose said.

Snow nodded. Then they found their way back to their abandoned baskets of branches and pinecones and started making their way home.

"We shouldn't tell Mama about this," Rose said, looking around as if their mother might be standing right behind them. "Like we didn't tell about the library or the Little Man. Our rule." Rose's hands had finally stopped shaking. "She's already so sad." Rose brushed a few bits of brown fur from her sleeve. "And I'm not sure she'd believe us, anyway."

"Do you think the objects from the library make things happen?" Snow asked.

Rose linked her arm with Snow's and gave her a doubtful look. "There must be a reason the key worked."

"I think there's something special about that key, about all the things in the library. The Librarian called them 'stories.' What about your scissors? What could their story be?"

When they got home, Snow showed their mother the key so she could prove to Rose that it was meant for the trap.

"It's a skeleton key," her mother said, nodding. "A special kind. It opens any lock."

"Oh," Snow said, frowning.

Rose thought, *And that's the reason.*

Their mother looked at them. "Where did you get this, anyway, my wandering girls?" She held the key in her palm, turning it over curiously. "I wonder what else you find out there." All of a sudden, she gathered them up in her arms and squeezed them tightly. "Now, what should we have for dinner?" she asked, drifting off to the kitchen.

That night Snow and Rose sat on the edges of their beds. "We need to bring this to Ivo tomorrow," Rose said, tying closed the invitation to Snow's party with a small piece of string.

"But after that—" Snow rifled around in the drawer

of the little bedside table. She produced the playing card, with its nine stars, and held up the key in her other hand. "Back to the library."

x x x

"It's close." Rose looked down at the notes she'd made the first time they came. They crossed over to the other side of the path, heading east.

"Let me be sure, then," Ivo said, scanning the trees as they flicked by. "You said it's somewhere aboveground?"

When they mentioned the library to Ivo, Snow and Rose were surprised to find he had no idea what they were talking about. He had never heard of the tall, narrow building full of stories. But that day, his parents gave Ivo a free afternoon with no chores at the farm, no foraging to do, and he could go with them.

"Well . . . ," Rose said, trailing off. She didn't want to say too much, because she wanted him to be surprised, as they'd been.

Snow took off ahead. "It's best if we just show you," she called behind her. Then she turned back to Rose and Ivo. "I think I hear a goat!"

Ivo looked at Rose, his face a question mark.

"I can't believe we know something here that you don't," Rose said.

"You might know this one place, but I know the woods," Ivo said, his voice defensive. "This library mustn't have been here long."

"It *looks* like it's been here forever," Rose said. And then, all of a sudden, there they were, at the path that led to the narrow little house. They walked past the sign, the painted hand creaking as it swung.

Rose knocked on the heavy door. This time it didn't open on its own. The three waited and heard nothing. Snow shifted her feet, impatient, then knocked again.

They saw a flicker of movement at the small window beside the door, frosted in the corners with thick gray dust. The very top of the Librarian's face looked out at them and then vanished again. It was another minute before they heard uneven footsteps thumping behind the door, then the noisy metal sound of one, two, three locks unlatching.

The Librarian peered around the door and straight over the children's heads, her eyes darting one way and then the other.

Rose cleared her throat and said hello with a shy wave.

"Hello," the Librarian said, swinging the door open. They followed her into the house, and she locked all three locks behind them. "Can't be too careful," she said. "Not these days."

Snow, Rose, and Ivo exchanged looks.

"Well, you're back!" the Librarian said, smiling. "And you've brought a new patron, I see!"

Just as Ivo said, "Pleased to meet you," a small tan goat wandered up to him and began chewing his sweater sleeve. Rose rescued Ivo by wedging herself between him and the goat.

"Go on!" said the Librarian. "We've added new stories since your last visit."

The children looked up at the staircase, lined with its hundreds of tiny shelves.

The Librarian wandered to her office, where she started adding to wobbly stacks on the floor in an attempt to make some space. "Let me know if I can help you," she called out. "Or if you have any returns."

"I'm just going to look," Ivo said, and started up the staircase. The girls went to the Librarian's desk.

"One return," Snow said, and produced the key, placing it in the Librarian's lined palm. The woman polished the key on the sleeve of her sweater and tossed it into a tin box at her feet, where it landed with a *clink*.

"But we also have a question," Rose said.

The Librarian nodded, then began rummaging through her desk, looking for something.

"It's about the—" Snow started, then stopped, waiting.

The Librarian appeared only to be half listening as she tossed things this way and that.

Snow's voice grew impatient. "It's about the stories."

"Please," added Rose.

"There they are!" the Librarian announced. She produced another beat-up tin like the one that had held the cookie crumbs last time. This time it was filled with a hodgepodge of candy, some wrapped, some unwrapped. "Please," she said, offering the tin to the girls.

"About the stories," Rose repeated firmly as she eyed the candy. A few of the pieces looked suspiciously nibbled on. Snow reached in and unwrapped a peppermint.

"Mmm-hmm," the Librarian said, nodding. "Yes, what about them?"

"The things in your library—the stories—do you know what will happen in them?" Rose asked. She felt sure of the answer, but she wanted Snow to hear it.

"I'm not sure I understand," the Librarian said.

The little black goat appeared and began to finish off the contents of the candy tin. The Librarian shooed the goat, but it didn't budge.

Ivo interrupted, calling down from somewhere high up on the staircase. "I think this is a button I lost!"

Snow, Rose, and the Librarian all looked up.

"Maybe, maybe not," the Librarian called back. She

turned back to the girls and smiled. "Yes, my dear? You were saying?"

"Well, what if I wanted a specific story about— about finding someone," Snow began, looking at Rose, then back at the Librarian. "Could I check out a story like that?"

The Librarian shook her head. "It doesn't work that way."

Snow fished around in her pocket. "Here, I have my card."

Ivo's voice interrupted again. "And I think this whistle is mine, too!" A thin *doot-doot* sound followed from the staircase. "Papa carved it for me, and I must have lost it somewhere. . . ."

As the Librarian shouted up to Ivo again, "Maybe, maybe not," Rose looked at Snow and saw her sister's eyes filling with disappointment. Rose had been sure she was right about the key. That there *was* an explanation; there always was. But somewhere inside her, hidden in a corner, was a part that wanted to be wrong.

"Right, so what was it you wanted to know?" The Librarian turned back to the girls seated in front of her.

Snow stood quietly, scowling at the worthless conversation. She looked at Rose, their feet shifting through wayward piles.

The whistle sounded again, louder this time. They turned to find Ivo waiting for them.

"So how does this work, then?" Ivo said.

The Librarian began the process of finding her box of cards. As she looked, she explained that with his library card, he could check things out, anything he'd like. Ivo was too polite to argue with her about *what* exactly belonged to *whom,* so he just took his card and whistle.

"Do you want to go up the stairs and look for something else?" Rose asked Snow.

"That's okay," Snow said with a sigh.

They headed toward the front door, the tan and black goats trailing them, both trying to get a bite of one of Rose's braids.

As the Librarian unlatched the door and the children filed out, Ivo whistled twice and said, "Thanks, then."

"You're welcome anytime," the Librarian said. "Well, not anytime. The right time, you know."

They said their goodbyes, and Snow, Rose, and Ivo started down the path.

The old woman called out, "One more thing!" The children stopped and turned.

The Librarian looked at Rose, then at Snow, for a moment, clear-eyed and sharp and not at all the person she'd been just before. Her voice was certain and sure. "To find out what a story's *really* about," the Librarian said, "you don't ask the writer. You ask the *reader.*"

Snow looked at Rose in a way that asked, *What does that mean?* But then the little black goat charged out of the house and chased Ivo and the girls away through the trees. As they walked back toward the path, they could hear the Librarian shouting for the goat to come inside.

CHAPTER 9

A Birthday Party

The night before Snow's birthday, Rose couldn't sleep. She lay awake in the cold, listening to a sound she wasn't sure was there: the sound of the bear's pained roar.

Finally, she padded out to the dark kitchen to fetch some water and found the front door open. Just outside, in the chilly air, a stump of candle glowed. Their mother sat alone, wrapped in a thick sweater, her knees to her chest. A familiar smell hung around her, and a tendril of smoke rose before her. Rose didn't know whether it was one of the times her mother wanted to be left alone or if she should sit down beside her.

"Rosie?" her mother said, hearing or sensing her. "I'm worried about tomorrow." She twisted around, and Rose saw that she was smoking their father's old pipe.

Rose sat down next to her, surprised to see the pipe.

"I wish we could throw Snow a big, beautiful party. . . ." Her mother sighed. She smoothed Rose's bedtime hair. "But what's keeping *you* awake?" She exhaled a curl of smoke and gave Rose a half smile. "Snow, I can always tell what's wrong. She's like glass. Rose, you're like . . . something I can't see through. Wood, maybe. Or milk. Inscrutable. My inscrutable girl."

"It's nothing," Rose said. She didn't want to tell her mother about the bear sound. Or the bear. "I didn't know you . . ." Rose gestured to the pipe.

"Oh!" her mother said, laughing softly. She sounded embarrassed. "I don't know if it's because it calms me or because it reminds me of your father or . . . what, exactly." She breathed out a tiny plume of smoke, pale against the black night. "Probably both." She paused. "I'm doing all I can, Rosie."

Rose put her hand on her mother's. "Me too."

X X X

The next morning when the girls woke up, the main room of the cottage was a woodland version of the grand birthdays of their past. Rose held her breath as Snow's eyes traveled: In place of glass-glittered stars were berry branches and acorn bouquets tied up with ribbon. In place of silver streamers were pinecone garlands looping overhead. Instead of decadent piles of perfect little cakes, there was a simple butter cake, layered with preserves. Where a table would've been heaped with presents in extravagant wrappings, there were only two gifts, wrapped in brown paper and tied with blue string.

Snow turned to Rose. "Mama did all of this?" Her eyes went around the room again. "It's lovely." She smiled and nodded in appreciation.

Rose yawned. "I helped," she said, smiling sleepily. She leaned toward Snow and whispered, "And I used the library's little scissors to cut the ribbons. Maybe the scissors' story is about a birthday party."

Snow shook her head. "Last time we rescued a bear," she whispered. "They've got to be meant for something more exciting than a party."

Their mother appeared behind them, her hair combed and pinned up, her lips pink. Rose was surprised to see her this way after the night before, after the way she'd been for months and months. It was as if she'd been asleep for a very long time and had woken up one day, this day, eyes bright, wearing her prettiest dress.

"How've I been lucky enough to have you for ten whole years?" their mother said, wrapping her arms around Snow's shoulders.

There was a knock at the cottage door.

"Who could that be?" their mother said, swinging it open. Cool air and the smell of leaves filled the doorway.

Ivo waited politely, his spindly silhouette outlined in the bright sunlight. He carried his fiddle strapped to his back and clutched a small, lumpy parcel wrapped in cloth. Their mother thanked him before placing his gift on the table with the other two. "Come in," she said.

"Thank you, ma'am," Ivo said, wiping his shoes carefully before walking inside. "I can stay until dark," he added, his expression serious. Their mother nodded, returning his serious look.

"Did you find your way all right?" Rose asked.

Ivo nodded. "Your directions were good."

"I'm glad they let you come," Snow added.

Ivo's ears grew rosy. "Well, if it were up to my mum, I'd dig a tunnel to your house."

He gazed at the interior of the little cottage as if it were a grand hall that needed to be carefully appreciated. "I didn't know you lived somewhere so nice, then," he said, picking up the little brass elephant and holding it carefully in his hand. He passed the small bookcase, his fingertips thrumming across the spines of the books. He wandered around the room, admiring the table, running his hands over the quilts thrown on the back of a bench. His eyes and fingers didn't register the knotholes in the wood or the worn places in the fabric.

They spent the afternoon with music and games. Ivo was extremely good at shadow puppets. They drew the curtains and watched him cast dogs and rabbits on the wall, ending with a very lovely shadow swan.

And for the first time, Snow took her violin from its place on the shelf and played her favorite song. It was wistful and pretty, and even though some notes didn't sound right, she remembered more than she had forgotten. Then it was Ivo's turn, and he played them a jig, lively and fast, the kind made for dancing. When they were finished, Snow and Ivo bowed, and their audience clapped.

They had glasses of crab apple cider spiced with nutmeg and ate too many pieces of cake, and then it was time for presents.

Ivo's was a parcel of lumpy sweets, some red-spotted sugar, some covered in chocolate. "Candy mushrooms," he said. "There's not real mushrooms inside," he added, seeing Snow's face. "Mum makes them as a treat."

Two small stones tumbled out after the candy. "And two sparking stones," Ivo said, quickly adding, "They *are* real stones, *not* candy."

"What do they do?" Rose asked.

Ivo took the dark stones and struck them together. "Light your kindling wood . . ." Sparks flashed in the air, lighting up the table. Ivo placed a stone in Snow's hand. "And warm your pockets." The stone was smooth, and its comfortable warmth spread from her palm to her fingertips. She passed it around the table so everyone else could feel it.

"Thank you," Snow said, smiling as she bit the cap of a chocolate mushroom.

She unwrapped a bumpy and rough scarf that Rose had knitted out of pale gray wool.

"I promise I will make you something nicer when I'm better at it," Rose said, blushing. "I wanted to make you something pretty." She looked at the scarf, frowning. "But that is definitely not."

"It's . . . *interesting*," Snow said, valiantly trying to knot it around her neck. "It's . . . warm?"

"It's hideous!" Rose shouted, bursting into laughter. Everyone else laughed, too.

"I made you something warm, too, my Snowbell," their mother said, placing the last package in front of her.

Inside was a pale blue cape stitched out of soft wool.

"The color of your eyes," her mother added, with one of her rare smiles on her lips and in her voice.

Snow looked around then. "And . . . that's everything," she said.

They were all still smiling as Snow's own smile began to fade.

"Well, did you make your birthday wish?" her mother asked, trying to make the happy moment stay.

"Yes," Snow said, her voice growing quiet. Her eyes went far away, and she tried another smile, but the only one she could muster looked painted on. Her lip quivered, and a tear slid from the corner of her eye.

Rose could tell she was fighting against the thing that wanted to run away with her.

Snow blinked back her tears. "Thank you for the—" She paused and calmed herself. "Thank you for the lovely party," she finally finished. Then a familiar warm softness bumped against her leg, and Snow looked down to find another party guest. She smiled a real smile. "Earl Grey!" she said, wiping her eyes on her sleeve. But the cat hissed and swiped at Snow, then stalked under the table legs nervously.

"What's the matter with him?" Snow said. The cat darted from under the table and made jumpy circles around the room until finally he flopped down on the rug near the hearth and let out a yowl.

"Is he sick?" Rose asked. Their mother went over to the cat, who crouched, hissing at first, then reluctantly allowed himself to be scratched behind the ears. She frowned, then placed a hand gently on the cat's round belly. She stood and smiled at the three children. "The gentleman Earl Grey is going to have kittens."

Snow, Rose, and Ivo looked at one another, speechless.

"All this time, he was a girl!" Snow said incredulously. Both she and Rose repeated some variation of this at least a dozen times as they waited. They made a big nest of blankets on the rug to give the cat privacy and somewhere soft to rest. She lay hidden in the blankets, curled in on herself like a spiral shell.

The girls' mother made tea, and they watched the blankets so long that Rose almost fell asleep.

Finally, Earl the lady-cat began to yowl. Troubling sounds came from the blankets.

When all was calm, they approached the cloth nest, and gently, slowly, Snow pulled the top quilt aside. Curled against the big, soft pillow of Earl Grey's stomach were three tiny kittens, blind and slick-downed and squirming.

Everyone leaned in quietly to see them.

"Is that what they're supposed to look like?" Rose said in a hush.

"They look a bit like mice," Ivo whispered. "Don't you think?"

Earl Grey cleaned the babies diligently with her rough tongue. After their bath, they'd transformed into soft-eared balls of fluff, pink noses in the air, whipping their stubby tails this way and that, one black, one white, and one gray-striped like its mother.

"They're the sweetest things I've ever seen," Snow said. Then to the kittens, "Don't you worry about anything. We are going to take such good care of you." She looked at her mother. "We *can* keep them?"

"I—I don't know if we can keep all of them . . . ," she answered carefully. "Maybe one?"

"Maybe three!" Snow said. "There's a white kitten for me and a black one for Rose! It's meant to be." She gave her mother a pleading look. "And the gray one, well . . . we can't give any of them away!"

Her mother kissed Snow's head and said, "We'll see."

Snow threw her arms around her mother's waist. Rose smiled and went off in search of more blankets as Ivo eyed the twilight in the windows.

They all gathered at the door to say goodbye, watching him disappear into the deep blue woods.

When they came inside, Rose tried to help her mother clean, but she could barely keep her eyes open, so she climbed up to the loft and into bed. Snow made a bed near the hearth so she could sleep next to Earl Grey and her kittens. As she lay on her side, her face resting on a pillow beside the three soft little shapes, she whispered, "Happy birthday."

CHAPTER 10
The River Monster

After the birthday party, it rained for days. The weather snuffed out the momentary brightness in their mother, but Snow and Rose hardly noticed because now they had the kittens. Tiny mews, the cold patter on the roof, and the sound of water boiling for tea were all they heard. Finally, after their drowsy days cooped up, the sky cleared. Snow and Rose raced to see who could lace up her boots quickest. They kissed the kittens and left them in Earl Grey's care, then ran outside under a bright sky.

The rain had turned the crisp brown leaves slick

and black underfoot. The sisters' breath hung cold in the air as they set off to see Ivo.

They walked through the forest, down toward the stream. In her hurry to get outside, Rose had remembered her satchel but forgotten her cape until she saw Snow, warm in hers. Rose shivered in her sweater, and Snow noticed.

She reached into her pocket, looking proud, and fished out the stones Ivo had given her. She struck them together, and a brilliant flash lit the damp air, leaving a trace of blue smoke. Snow handed the stones to Rose. "You can use them."

Rose tucked a stone in each of her pockets, turning them deliciously warm.

The light was different, cold and bright—winter light. The trees were mostly bare, the last clinging leaves stripped away by the storm. When Snow and Rose reached the little stream they'd waded in during summer, it was different, too: the days of rain had turned it into something like a small river.

The sisters walked alongside as the water rushed past them over the rocks. They walked around a familiar bend, the river lapping high above its usual mark.

Suddenly, up ahead, they spied something thrashing in the water. They quickened their pace to see what it was. When they got closer, they found a monstrous fish, like a legless silver crocodile.

It looked ancient, its body covered in sharp fins and scales like plated metal. The fish was at least five feet long, uneasy in the shallow water, too big to be at home in a little forest stream.

Its jaw was clamped on another creature, another someone—a someone the girls were surprised to see again. The Little Man clung to the reeds at the water's edge, his bottom half kicking against the fish's mouth. The silver teeth snapped in the clear water, rows of needles studding the creature's great hinged jaw. The Little Man turned to face the fish, shrieking.

Snow looked at Rose with an expression that said, *Again?!*

The Little Man spotted the sisters on the shore. "Oh, lovely girls!" he gasped. His feet slid in the mud on the bank. He was halfway in the water now. "My rescuers!"

The fish, its bladed fins flashing in the light, caught the Little Man, and he was pulled completely underwater.

There was a change in the weather, and the bright sky clouded over. Rose looked up at the clouds, ready to turn back, but a thought crossed her mind: if they helped him again, he would have to offer them another

gift, another answer. She looked at Snow, both of them remembering his unpleasantness and riddles, weighing whether to help. Then threads of blood started to appear, like drops of red watercolor.

The girls clambered down the muddy bank to help, staining their stockinged knees. The Little Man struggled to hold his face above the water. "Please! I'm done for!" he cried before he was pulled under again. The water churned with limbs and silver scales. A small arm broke the surface of the water.

The girls braced themselves against some sturdy roots that jutted from the riverbank. Rose held Snow around the middle. Snow reached out to grab the tiny hand, clasping its fingers with her own.

They pulled with all their might, managing to yank the Little Man up enough to breathe. He gasped for air and waved his arms. His whole body was free from the fish's jaws, except for his beard, which was tangled in the long teeth. When Rose realized that the beard could not come loose, she had an idea. She fumbled in the satchel slung across her chest. Her fingers found the scissors from the library. "We'll have to cut him loose!" she called out to Snow.

"You mean let go?" Snow shouted back.

The Little Man shrieked.

"No! I've got the scissors," Rose called.

"I can't hold on much longer," Snow said. "Crumbs!" Cold water splashed her, stinging them both.

Rose stretched to hand the scissors to Snow, who wriggled one hand free. She grabbed the handles, and in a flash, the tiny blades sliced through the tangled beard. Snow fell backward into Rose's lap. The Little Man flew up onto the riverbank. Defeated, the fish swam away, fins cutting a furious silver line above the dark stones.

Then the man let out a howl.

His fingers grasped the air beneath his chin.

"Mutilated!" he shrieked. "My lovely whiskers!" He searched the ground nearby. "What have you done with them? Thieves, thieves!"

The girls brushed themselves off and stood.

"We cut your beard to save you," Rose said. "It will grow back."

Snow frowned. "You could stop yelling long enough to thank us."

"No!" the Little Man snapped. "No gratitude for savage girls!"

Rose's hands were almost numb from cold. She felt for the stones, grown cool in her pockets. When the sparks flared as she warmed them again, the Little Man leapt backward, shrieking, "Fire!"

This was the first time the girls had seen his

eyes truly full of fear. "Nothing more wicked," he murmured.

"We should just throw him back in the river," Snow said, looking at Rose for permission.

"Please, I'm sorry if we did something wrong," Rose said. "Before . . . before you said we could ask you a—"

"No! No answers!" he shouted. "No gifts!"

Rose's heart fell. "What about 'This is polite, this is not polite' . . . ?"

"*You* are not polite!" He clutched at the scraggly remains of his beard, then turned and started away.

Before he could get far, Snow ran and caught him by his bony shoulder. "You just wait a MINUTE!" she said, her voice climbing with each word until she was hollering.

Rose ran to them and crouched down.

"You said you know everything in the woods?" Rose looked into his golden eyes. "Our father was traveling here, and he . . ."

"Get on with it!" the Little Man yelled, trying to jerk his shoulder free.

"He never came home," Snow added, tightening her grip.

"I thought—" Rose's voice grew desperate. "Is there anything you know? He rode a chestnut horse."

The Little Man finally snatched his shoulder free, and Snow crossed her arms.

"If you wanted to ask what the woods know," the Little Man said, narrowing his eyes, "what *I* know, you shouldn't have mangled me." He turned back to Rose and leaned closer. He was all wrinkles and bones, but he was luminous. Old and young, all at once.

Rose could feel his breath, cold as the winter air.

"You'd be wise never to cross my path or lay your hands on me again," he hissed. His voice was low and dangerous as he whispered, "Perilous am I."

With that, the man leapt away, looking for all the world like an overgrown grasshopper.

Rose began to cry, and it began to rain again.

The girls stood looking at each other, covered in mud.

"I didn't notice his legs before," Snow said.

"Me neither." Rose's voice was hollow. No matter how much she tried to reason it away, she had seen something she couldn't truly understand. "I don't think they bend the right way."

CHAPTER 11
Things with Teeth

The rain pattered all around them, landing cold on their heads and rolling off their cheeks. Rose was quiet as Snow stomped and fumed.

"Well, I don't care what's got him next time." They turned when they came to the forest of tall ferns, and made their way to Ivo's tree. "I don't care if a dragon's got him. . . . It can drag him down to—"

"Hello," Ivo said. He was wearing a fur hat and standing beneath the big, twisty tree that grew above his farm. "I heard you shouting from all the way down below."

Snow eyed his hat.

Ivo looked up as if he'd forgotten he was wearing it. "Oh!" he said, remembering. "I was helping my uncle." Ivo gestured to the glossy fur. "We were off at a market for a few days. That's what I've been up to, then." Ivo's narrow face beamed with pride.

Then his smile faded as he noticed the girls' muddy knees and stained clothes. "What have *you* been up to?"

The girls looked at each other and then back at Ivo. They both started speaking at once. Their words tumbled over each other as they furiously told their friend about the gigantic silver crocodile-fish and the Little Man.

Ivo's eyes grew worried. "You've got to be careful," he said, his forehead wrinkling. "I've told you Mum and Papa are worriers, but they're *right* to worry. Most times." He looked at Snow and Rose. "Why do you think we live underground?"

"That Little Man knows something," Rose said quietly. "Something about what's wrong with the woods. Though I'm not sure we're ever going to get him to tell."

"Some poor old fella," Ivo said, waving the thought away. "Probably harmless. Bandits, you steer clear of. But it's the beasts you watch out for. My uncle says there are more and more all the time. . . ." He looked at them. "If you see one or hear one, you run."

"I don't know if it's just the animals," Snow said. "It feels like there might be something else."

Ivo nodded. "Mum calls them 'in-betweens.' Like something is watching, but there's nothing there. You can't see them. But they're harmless, the in-between things." Ivo spoke with a certainty that meant there was no room for disagreement. "The ones to worry about are the things with teeth."

"Well, we've survived so far," Snow said, lifting her chin.

"Why are you only telling us this now?" Rose tried to brush away Ivo's superstition. Then she thought of the giant frog, staring. She thought of the Little Man's legs.

"I did tell you, a little," Ivo said. "But I didn't want to scare you." His face was serious. "You're not used to it here. It's always worse when the cold comes."

The girls shivered in their wet clothes.

Ivo noticed, and his face softened. "Better come inside and get dry. There's a pot of good cider."

He turned to the tree and pulled a branch—the lever that opened the door in the ground. He started down the hidden stairway that led to the farm. "Just be careful," he said. "Sometimes things aren't the way they seem."

Even underground, Rose felt a chill in her bones that the sparking stones couldn't warm away. It was made of unanswered questions, of things she didn't understand. Circling that coldness were thoughts about the Little

Man and his backward legs and the way he glowed. About these woods, wild and shifting. Her sense that everything here—big and small, predator and prey— everything could be dangerous.

X X X

Later, Ivo walked them home, the three huddled under one old umbrella. When they got to the cottage, Snow and Rose said nothing of their day. Their mother made dinner. The house was quiet until late at night, when a ferocious pounding thundered on the door and the walls of the cottage shook.

Everyone was startled awake by the sound, a great, heaving *Thump! Thump! Thump!*

It came again, even louder.

The girls followed their mother, all three in their nightclothes. She motioned for them to stay close behind her. Outside the windows, there was only black.

"Who is there?" their mother called out in a different voice from her own, low and serious even as it wavered.

A huge shape moved past the black window.

Then a terrible clawing sound began on the door.

"Who is it?" their mother called again. She grabbed a knife from the kitchen drawer; Snow, a pair of shears. Rose stood behind them, brandishing the broom.

Silence answered. No thumping, no clawing.

Their mother, fierce and frail in her silk robe, threw back her shoulders and gripped the knife at her side. Another moment passed. Still silence.

She folded the girls behind her, as if hidden in her wings, Snow with her shears and Rose with her broom. Then their mother opened the door.

All that came in was a gust of cold night air.

Then, staggering, stumbling, came the bear. He didn't enter so much as fall, halfway through the open door, his body huge but weak.

Their mother walked backward and hugged the girls to her side, all three feeling a wary sadness that comes from seeing something mighty and wild cut down.

The bear's wound from the trap had gotten worse. He came forward, thrusting his front paws upward before thundering them to the ground. His claws left deep grooves in the soft wood of the floor.

Edith charged forward, brandishing her knife in her hand. She held it before the bear. "Go away," she said in warning.

The bear raised its head, and they faced each other. He breathed in a fierce snort.

"Get out," she said.

The bear bellowed back, bleak and low.

She raised the knife.

"Stop!" the girls called. They ran between the bear and their mother.

"We know him," Snow said. "We saved him once." She knelt beside him, her hand on his gigantic head.

Their mother looked from Snow to Rose, then back again.

"He's hurt," Rose pleaded. She eyed the trail of blood that followed him.

"Girls . . . ," their mother said, her mouth open to form words she couldn't find. Instead, she just shook her head.

"Mama?" Snow said. She saw the bear's bad leg tremble, and tears beaded in her eyes.

Before their mother could fumble for an answer, the bear sighed so violently it seemed like the very life of him had gone gusting out. He collapsed with a shuddering crash.

While the three of them tried to agree on a plan for this bear in their doorway, Earl Grey had come quietly into the kitchen. They watched, surprised, as the cat approached the bear, sniffing calmly. Her kittens were hidden away somewhere, but Earl Grey was not afraid.

Their mother decided that if Earl Grey didn't fear him, this huge animal, that must mean something. They managed to rouse the bear long enough to lead him to the living room, where he fell again.

They watched as Earl Grey fetched her kittens from their hiding place, returning them to their place by the hearth. She settled them one by one.

They made a fire, and Snow drew closer to the bear's warm body. His breathing was shallow, and his eyes were closed. "Bears shouldn't even be out now, right?" Snow asked. "They should be in their caves to sleep away winter."

"Why were you still out there?" Rose asked him. "What happened to you?"

"Let's just see if he makes it through the night," their mother said, yawning. "I wonder who else you've met out there. This is your second"—she raised her eyebrow at the bear—"guest."

When the sun began to rise, there was nothing left to do but try and sleep: Snow and Rose in their beds, their mother watchful and restless on the couch. Earl Grey and the kittens were piled warmly together on the rug nearby. The bear lay before the fireplace, his body rising and falling in sleep, as if someone had breathed life into the biggest bearskin rug there ever was.

CHAPTER 12

The Foragers' Feast

The bear stayed in his place near the fire. Snow
bandaged his leg in clean rags each day.

He seemed to grow stronger, even though he slept
for all but a few hours a day. The kittens began to venture closer to his giant paws, inching forward before
skittering away, back to their mother. The whole family
watched him, hoping he would stay tame and safe, hoping he would get better.

But the day came when they had to leave him alone.
The girls and their mother left the cottage in the late
morning, dressed in their warm capes. As they walked

through the bars of sunlight that streamed into the cold woods, they decided the bear must stay a secret.

"Not a mention of him," their mother said. "Not to *anyone.*"

Snow and Rose nodded. They knew just what Ivo would say, how he'd scold them.

The family made their way to a place the girls had been above but never inside: the Underground House. Rose led them, remembering all their searches for the hidden door.

Today the door was cleared of the moss and leaves that usually hid it away. It stood open, marked with a friendly white ribbon and a sprig of blue spruce, and music and voices floated up. Ivo waited by the door, and they followed him down to the tunnels and snug chambers that twisted underground, where no one could hear the wind that shook the bare trees above.

Just before the winter solstice, before Christmas came, the Underground House was warmed with a blazing fire, and a great table was set for the people of the woods. There, the people who lived hidden from the eyes of the village gathered around the wild gifts of the forest.

Snow and Rose wandered through the big room. It was spare but cozy. Roots curled and looped along the walls; dark planks of roughhewn wood covered the floor. Light beamed thinly through windows in the ceiling, falling onto simple furnishings. Lanterns and candles were gathered in groups on tables and shelves carved into the walls of earth.

The neighbors welcomed them: first Ivo's father, who nodded at them, his brown hair threaded with gray. Around him were uncles and aunts and a few other scattered strangers. Rose wondered where they all lived and if all their houses were hidden. The Librarian appeared in the small crowd.

"I told my mum about her," Ivo whispered.

The Librarian spied them and hobbled over. "I never asked, but how did your stories end?" She nibbled on a dark bread roll. "Or *did* they end?"

Rose thought about the key and the scissors. "Well . . ."

"They were like when knights rescue fair maidens," Snow said, looking sideways at Rose. "Only no knights, and the maidens weren't the ones who needed rescuing."

The Librarian nodded and took another bite of her bread. "Well, there are always more," she said. Then she straightened her back and smiled before thumping off, her steps uneven on the planks of the floor.

Ivo's mother stepped out of the kitchen. She was round and rosy, but her eyes were the same as Ivo's. She wore her brown hair tied up, and she hugged each of them tightly, especially Snow. (Ivo's mother was one of those people who hug harder when they sense someone resisting.)

An old man with wild bluish-gray hair came to hug them, too, but Ivo swooped in. "You don't know them, Uncle Vincent," he said, blushing as he steered the man away.

Ivo apologized and led Snow and Rose to the table hewn of wood, worn smooth with use. It stretched nearly the length of the room and was lined on either side with mismatched place settings and chairs. The center of the table was crowded with a bowl of dark mulled wine, as well as smooth wooden platters and bowls that Ivo's father had made, all piled with the food of the forest. The girls followed their friend around the table, and Ivo listed as he pointed: "Mushroom stew, mushroom soufflé, mushroom medley . . ."

"So, all mushrooms," Snow said.

"There's a dandelion salad," Ivo said. "Acorn stuffing . . . some nice wild onions. And quail eggs," he added, gesturing to a bowl of speckled eggs much smaller than Goldie the chicken's. "I'll show you your seats."

Rose was beside Snow, with Ivo across the table. Their mother sat next to Ivo's mother, down the table with the other grown-ups. Rose and Snow and Ivo were the only children there.

The other guests cheered suddenly as a man entered the dining room, setting aside his bow and quiver of arrows. He was striking, like the wildest person on earth, and he wore the coats of wild things. His cap was made from the feathers of a dozen birds: a thrush's spotted brown and a jay's brilliant blue and a snow owl's white and a magpie's black. From his belt hung a sheathed knife and a dark suede pouch.

He slung a roasted boar onto the waiting carving board at the very center of the table.

The man sat down right across from Rose, next to Ivo. When he was seated, Rose could see that he hid a slight frame under his furs. She didn't mean to stare, but she had seen the man before, sometime, somewhere. She looked at the arrows he leaned against the wall, the blue-feathered ends, circled in brass rings.

"My uncle Osprey," Ivo said, as if he were introducing a king.

The man felt Rose's eyes on him. He turned from his cup of mulled wine and looked back at her. He raised his eyebrows, and his eyes sparked with recognition. "We've met before." He smiled and glanced at Snow.

Rose elbowed Snow. Snow elbowed her back.

"You'd think two well-born girls would know the one who saved you," he chided.

At that moment, Rose realized who he was. "From the wolves," she and the man said in unison.

"Wolves!" Ivo exclaimed.

"A pack was after them," the man said. "I found these two sparrows up in a tree." He looked back at the girls. "That's where we met."

Snow eyed the tall bow.

"You met the greatest huntsman in the woods," Ivo said.

"Oh, I'm not so great, then," the man said, ruffling Ivo's hair.

"There's nothing he can't hit, even from a hundred yards away," Ivo said. "'No beast he cannot fell,' Papa says."

"But where would I be without my right hand?" the Huntsman said. "Actually, all this buttering-up reminds me: I have something for you." The man reached into a hidden pocket of his coat and retrieved a small bag, which was bound with a blue feather, the same as the ones on the ends of his arrows.

The bag jingled as it landed in Ivo's hands. The boy looked inside and pulled out a trio of gold coins, holding them for all to see.

Ivo's eyes lit up. "It's too much, this."

"You earned it, boy," the Huntsman said. "Nothing to make a fuss about." He patted Ivo on the back.

Ivo looked at his uncle. "Thank you." He stood and tied the pouch to his belt, so it swung from his hip like his uncle's.

When everyone finished eating, Ivo's mother brought out honeycomb cake, cider for the children, and mugs of hot coffee for the adults. When they finished their dessert, Ivo asked if he and the girls could be excused.

"Do you want to see my room?" He hoisted a small lantern.

As they left the table, Rose's ears caught a word: *monster.* Rose held Snow and Ivo back, hidden behind a wall. The adults had begun a serious conversation in low voices. The children stood outside the dining room, listening silently.

"Now that the little ones are gone, we can talk about the grave things that need talking about," Ivo's father said.

"There are monsters in these woods," the Huntsman began. There were murmurs and "yeses" and "indeeds" in agreement. The Huntsman continued. "The Menace of the Woods, some call it."

The children leaned closer to hear.

"And far too many that go missing because of 'em!" Ivo's father said.

"Monsters?" Rose heard her mother's voice speak. She sounded incredulous. "What do you mean?"

"Exactly what I say, my lady," the Huntsman said, his voice grave. "Monsters roam the woods. Beasts much bigger than nature intended."

"Ivo told me what the girls saw!" his mother said, almost whispering. "A monster in the stream, he said!"

"I don't know anything about—" Rose heard her mother begin, but her voice was drowned out. Rose knew her mother must be thinking of all the secrets they might be keeping from her.

The Librarian chimed in, her voice sadder than Snow and Rose had heard before. "And always worse when the cold comes."

"They're hungry now," Ivo's father said.

The Librarian went on. "A huge bear came around my house, and the next thing I know?"

Rose's heart caught in her chest. *The bear.*

Snow grabbed her hand.

"Daisy's gone! All he left was bones," the old woman continued, a waver in her voice. "I don't know how much longer I can stay. I've got my goats to think about."

"Goats!" Ivo's great-uncle Vincent repeated. "It could be *you!*"

"I saw the bear once," Ivo's mother said. "Could've

swallowed me whole. When did you last hear of a bear in these woods?"

"I know that bear. The King Bear, I call him," the Huntsman said. "He knows my trap. And I'll finish him off, I swear it."

Rose thought of the trap and its cruel metal jaws. She thought of the bear back at the cottage, asleep. She wanted to rush into the room where the grown-ups were speaking. But what would she say? What did she know? She didn't know if the bear was dangerous, only that he hadn't been a danger, not to them, not so far.

The Huntsman spoke again. "And who will they come for next? After goats and chickens, it will be the children. Hiding isn't enough anymore. We must protect ourselves!"

Murmurs of agreement went up.

"Any sightings, you let me know," the Huntsman said. "I will do the rest."

Rose murmured to Snow and Ivo, "Why doesn't anyone try to figure out *why* there are such big animals in the first place? Maybe it's something they eat. Maybe it's the water. There must be a reason."

Snow whispered, "Do you really think this is a *reason*able place?"

"If there *is* a reason, I want to know it," Ivo said.

"But I want us safe, most of all. My uncle will keep us safe."

Loud cheers of "Hear, hear!" for the Huntsman came from the dining room.

Rose felt sick in a way that had nothing to do with mushroom soufflé and everything to do with the uncertainty that tumbled in her stomach.

"If we could find the Little Man again," Snow said, "maybe we could *make* him tell us. We could threaten to throw him to the b—" Snow stopped short of giving away their fugitive at home.

Ivo hadn't noticed Snow's slip or Rose's look. "My uncle will keep us safe," he repeated, trying a match over and over until his face lit up with the sudden glow of the lantern. "Well, come along, then," he said, motioning down the hallway. "Remember, I wanted to show you something."

CHAPTER 13

What Ivo Found

Ivo's room wasn't as much a room as it was a small, rough hollow carved out of the wall, like a person-sized shelf. Tucked inside was a mattress stuffed with hay, a pillow, and a little shelf holding a comb, a pair of socks, and a dented tin box.

Ivo reached for the tin box and opened it with a look of pride.

"I wanted to show you this, then. My favorite thing." He held out the box. "My most beautiful thing."

The girls stared silently at the object in the tin box.

At the handle made of ivory carved with a delicate bird.

At the bright polished silver.

At their father's knife.

Ivo hung it on his belt next to the pouch of gold coins. He looked at the girls, smiling and expectant. "It's nice, then, isn't it? Almost as nice as the things at your house."

Rose felt sick all over again. She struggled to get her words out while the weight of everything unknown pressed down.

"What's the matter?" Ivo asked. "Only a knife."

Snow's voice was cold and low. "How did you get that?"

Ivo's smile fell. "I—I found it." His soft voice took on a sharp edge.

"When?" Rose asked. "And where? Where did you find it?"

"What business is it of yours *where* I found it?" Ivo said. The tips of his ears were red.

"It belonged to—" Rose began.

"It belongs to our *father*!" Snow shouted.

"What do you mean? I found it on the ground. Just lying there." Ivo's eyebrows were furrowed as he backed away. "I didn't steal it, if that's what you're thinking!"

Snow scowled at Ivo. Rose stared at the knife.

"On the ground?" Snow said, eyeing him suspiciously. Ivo nodded.

"What *else* did you find?"

"Nothing," Ivo said.

"Well, what else do you *know*?" Rose asked, hopeful. "Anything could help. Anything."

"I swear," Ivo said, his voice losing its edge, "I only know what you told me." He looked Rose in the eyes before turning to Snow and doing the same. "Your father took the path and never come back."

Snow's dark scowl began to lift.

"I'm sorry," Ivo said.

There was a long silence before Snow said, "You didn't do anything wrong."

Rose took a few steps toward him and wrapped her arms around his narrow shoulders, and Ivo hugged back.

"If it belonged to him, then"—Ivo took the knife off his belt—"it belongs to you." Hesitation flickered across his face, but he placed the knife firmly in Rose's hand.

The girls looked at each other, uncertain they were ready for the answer to the question they needed to ask. "Will you show us where you found it?" Snow said.

"Of course." Ivo nodded and straightened his shoulders. "Of course I will." He led them back out of the tunnel, all three walking with purpose.

There was only one way in and out of Ivo's house, so they had to pass through the party to get aboveground.

They wove their way back to the dining room quietly. The grown-ups had gathered near the fire, where Ivo's mother played the accordion. Afternoon sun fell from the windows in narrow gold beams around her.

Snow and Rose found their mother and pulled her aside, letting her know they would walk home with Ivo, who was trying his best to sneak away unnoticed.

They finally reached the stairs, when Ivo's great-uncle Vincent wandered up.

"Do you see them?" he asked, his white hair glowing in the firelight, like dandelion fluff.

"See what?" Snow asked, inching away.

"Up there," the man said, pointing at one of the round windows set into the ceiling. "Outside."

The children looked up to the stream of light that filtered through the window.

"Is it snowing?" Ivo asked. The window framed the bare branches sketched across the pale sky, nothing more or less. Ivo waved silently to his uncle as they crept quietly up the stairs and opened the front door. "Sometimes he sees things that aren't there," Ivo whispered.

Aboveground, no snowflakes drifted in the air. Ivo hurried out in front of the girls, looking for the place he'd found the knife.

Snow turned to Rose, whispering as they walked. "Did *you* see them?"

"What do you mean?" Rose said. "Snowflakes?"

Snow frowned. "No." She looked at her sister. "I think they were fairies."

Rose sighed. The importance of their expedition, of what they might find, was all she could think of.

"Rose." Snow caught her sister's sleeve. "I think the woods might—" She paused, looking around. "I think the woods might be enchanted."

"You sound like Ivo," Rose whispered, walking faster. She felt for the knife in her pocket. "Keep up."

"But what about everything that's happened?" Snow said, lagging a few paces behind.

"Ivo's family doesn't read," Rose went on, ignoring Snow's question. "People who don't read books believe in superstition."

Snow quickened her steps, crossing in front of Rose with a loud, trailing whisper. "Superstitions have to come from somewhere."

The sun was sinking low between the trees as Ivo led them to the place. It was a place they'd been before, where they'd picked blackberries that first day they left the path. When they didn't know the woods, any of it. Ivo showed them where he'd found the knife, on the ground beside the green brambles, now a maze of brown thorns.

"Are you sure this is the right spot?" Rose asked,

her eyes searching the bramble patch for anything that might be a clue.

"Right here," Ivo said, pointing to an ordinary spot of forest floor.

"Did you see anything *else*?" Rose asked, hunting and sifting through brittle leaves and branches. Snow waded halfway into a tangled hedge, not caring when the dried thorns caught her cape or scratched her hands. Ivo knelt nearby, looking into the scraggly underbrush.

He fidgeted with the socks on his hands, remembering the bloodstains he'd cleaned off the knife. He wouldn't tell them about that. He would never tell them about that.

"Let's look carefully," said Rose. "Just in case there's anything, no matter how small."

So they spread out. They stooped low and climbed up and peered under fallen trees. Once the girls both gave a little shout, when they thought they had the beginnings of some clue, but there was never anything except the forest floor. They circled each other as they searched the thicket, but it was cold, and the light was fading quickly.

It was nearly dark when they came back together, empty-handed. "We can look again when it's light," Ivo offered.

Rose took the knife from her pocket and looked at it.

"I'm sorry," Ivo said again.

Ivo walked with them until the cottage was in sight, and with defeated, tired goodbyes, they parted ways. The girls could hear the coins in his pouch jingling as he walked away, leaving the path and starting through the trees. Rose worried about him setting off alone. Then she reminded herself that he had done this the night of Snow's party, and he'd made it home.

Ivo knew the way between the cottage and his own house. He tried not to worry that the sky was growing dark and the shadows were growing long.

One shadow in particular watched Ivo. It moved on legs that bent backward, flickering behind the boy as he walked quickly through the skinny birches and the big, winding oaks. A scattering of real snowflakes began to fall, and though the snow was silent, Ivo stopped and stood and listened, as if he heard something. Then he shivered and quickened his pace.

The shadow followed. It waited and it watched. But it was too late to run. The shadow found Ivo, and Ivo never found his way home.

WHAT THE TREES WORRIED

"You were seen," the old one scolded.

"Oh, it harms nothing," the young one said. "Nobody believes her."

"When you are careless, you endanger us all," the old one said.

"But I watch them because I'm waiting," the young one said impatiently, the sound of a sapling shivering in the wind. "When will it happen?"

"You cannot be seen," the old one said in a voice low and grave, uncoiling like the innermost rings of an ancient tree. "And you cannot make it happen."

"But I can help," the young one said. "Someday, I will."

CHAPTER 14

The Beast and the Bandits

In the five days that followed, the woods were covered in white. Snow and Rose watched from the windows as the flurries that began on the night of the feast grew into a blizzard. They made sure Goldie was tucked safely in her coop with extra food and wood shavings for her bed. Nobody ventured out. When they opened the front door to the frozen air, their noses weren't nipped; they were bitten.

In the bear's time by the hearth, with Snow as his nurse, his wound healed. He began to stand and stretch and roll around drowsily on the floor before falling back into his deep bear sleep. As mornings turned into nights and the house went on around him, he slept and slept, a kind of halfway hibernation.

And every morning and night, the sisters fed the bear, as they had since he came. When Snow fed him, she ruffled his fur and smoothed his ears. Sometimes she sneaked a brown egg into the bowl she laid by his side. But when Rose fed the bear, she walked with tentative steps and never got too close, even though he looked at her with kind eyes and Snow called her a coward.

The kittens were as unafraid as Snow. They dashed out of their hiding places to jump on the bear, climbing the back of their warm napping mountain. They trusted his gentleness, even though Rose couldn't. She couldn't shake the thought that, even with the gentleness, he could've been the reason *why*.

Their mother looked on, her eyes watchful. She thought of the old peasant stories she'd heard, first as a child and then repeated at the feast. But the way the kittens and Earl Grey trusted the bear, and the way the girls cared for him—these were good things. That was all she could be certain of.

The snowstorm broke on the fifth day. After the bear had eaten his sleepy breakfast, the girls pushed the door open, knocking icicles to the ground. The cold air rushed in. The bear lumbered to his feet and came to their side. He was strong, and his stride was steady.

"Come on," Snow said, closing the door and grabbing her cape. She turned to the bear. "We need to see if that leg of yours is really healed."

Rose looked at her. "Is this a good idea?"

Snow patted the fur that rolled on the back of the bear's neck, and answered her sister with a proclamation: "We are going for a walk."

"We can't go far," Rose said, her voice a whisper. She was thinking of the Huntsman's vow.

"That's the thing," Snow said, smiling. "*No one* will be out."

Rose nodded. "But we won't go far," she repeated, her voice firm as she pulled on her mittens and cape.

Snow nodded back, and the sisters and the bear stepped outside.

The woods had changed, transformed into a palace of ice that shone like glass and glittered white and silver. As they walked, their boots plunged deep into soft banks of snow. The bear's limp was invisible. Rose and Snow walked on either side as he padded along. Sometimes he broke into a slow gallop. Sometimes he nuzzled his snout in the snow, obviously happy to be somewhere bigger than a tiny cottage.

The girls played hide-and-seek in the banks and

behind fallen trees, gathering ammunition and then pelting each other (and sometimes the bear) with snowballs. When they tossed one to the bear, he tried to catch it in his mouth. He towered on his hind legs to catch them, snapping his mouth shut, running in a victorious circle when he caught one.

In this way, they threaded a route through the trees, bare except for draped white coats. Even Rose forgot that they weren't supposed to go too far. It felt as if they were the only things alive in the quiet and the white. Then suddenly they found themselves at the edge of the winter woods, and they were not alone.

The bear heard the voices first. His ears perked up, and he froze where he stood. Then the girls heard the voices, too.

They looked out through the trees and saw the encampment. The bandits had returned to the hillside from the empty barn where they'd stolen shelter. The break in the storm had brought them out, hoping the clear sky would mean an anxious traveler with deep pockets. They drank from tin cups and warmed their hands around a fire. A charred rabbit twisted on the spit.

The girls stood on either side of the bear, all three inside the columns of trees, facing the campsite at the edge of the woods.

It was too late to hide.

"Will you look what we have here?" called one of the bandits, a tall man in black. "Two little maids, out walking their pet." The men stood, eyeing the bear, their hands ready at their weapons.

"That's the King Bear," said another. Rose recognized him from their last encounter, a small man in a tattered gray uniform. "There's a pretty ransom to the one who brings back that monster's head," he continued. His voice rose, excited by the prospect.

A man in blue, younger than the other two, pulled a long hunting knife, silver and toothed, from the leather sheath at his waist.

"You don't know anything about him!" Snow cried out over the white banks.

"Snow!" Rose hushed her sister, even as she knotted her own fists. She didn't know if they could outrun the men again.

The man in gray looked at Rose. "I know your face, girl." He took in Rose's weathered satchel, their worn boots, the dresses they had nearly outgrown. "But you are much changed."

The bear let out a low growl as the men drew closer.

The bandit in black stepped toward the sisters, a smile playing on his lips. "I'm sure there's someone who'd pay nicely to see you again," he called. "Might see a profit today after all."

The bear moved forward, showing his teeth.

The bandit stooped so he was at eye level with the girls. "Should we see what kind of bounty we can get for one King Bear and two cubs?"

Snow and Rose backed away farther into the trees.

The bandit in gray came to his side. "Perhaps we let the little misses run along," he said, his voice quiet.

"Grab 'em," the black bandit replied, jerking his head at the girls. "Kill the bear," he said to the young man in blue.

"Run!" Rose screamed. She turned and pulled Snow back into the woods.

The blue bandit swung his knife, but the bear swung his paw, knocking the man to the ground. Then the bear took off, racing beside the girls. Even with the flicker of a limp in his step, his lumbering body was nimbler than his shape could ever suggest. The three ran, their legs cutting through the snow. But the snow hides many things, like the tangle of roots that caught Rose's foot. She shot forward, and her legs flew out behind her, with no time to catch herself on her palms. She slammed into the ground, her breath knocked out of her chest.

Snow turned to help her sister, shouting, "Get up!"

The bear heard and circled back. The bandits were almost upon them now.

Snow helped Rose stumble to her feet.

The bear stepped in front of the girls, a wall, a mountain. He let out a rumbling roar, and the skeleton trees around them trembled and rained snow. The bandits stepped back and looked at each other, the one in blue still gripping his knife. The bear knelt in the snow, as much as a bear can kneel. He lifted his head and looked at Snow and Rose. And they understood. They climbed onto his back, gripping his fur.

The bear turned and raced away with his riders.

The girls looked over their shoulders and saw the bandits growing smaller at the edge of the woods. The trees seemed to close behind them and open up before them, easing their way. The girls held on tightly, bumping and jostling as the bear thundered through the snowbanks,

back the way they'd come, where they'd played. Only when the cottage came into view did his pace begin to slow, approaching their door with a lumbering walk.

The girls slipped off his warm back and ran to open the door, where their mother waited for them inside. She eyed all three as they tumbled through the doorway.

The girls' faces were flushed and numb as they told her of nothing except their snowball fight. The bear limped to his place at the hearth, and it was clear that he shouldn't have run the way he did.

Their mother scattered snow to hide the big paw prints leading to the house, and when she was satisfied, she locked the door behind them.

X X X

They barely had time to warm their hands when there was a sharp knock at the door.

All the hearts in the cottage, big and small, jumped at the same time. Rose went to the window and peered out carefully. She motioned to Snow, and together they saw the Huntsman pacing in the white outdoors. Their mother walked to the door and held up her hands to silently ask, *Well?*

"Don't!" Rose whispered.

They looked back to where the bear slept by the hearth.

The Huntsman knocked again, this time calling, "Anyone there?"

Everyone held their breath, as if he could hear them through the walls. They waited as he knocked a third time, calling out once more, "I mean you no harm." His voice was growing impatient as he finally boomed, "I can see the smoke in your chimney."

After that, all was silence. They peered out to be sure that he had gone. His boots had left a new set of dark footprints in the snow.

That night, when Rose fed the bear, she approached him with her usual tentative steps. Snow was bandaging his leg. His old wound was bleeding again. She looked up as Rose hesitated. But Rose kept coming, drawing closer, unafraid. She put the bowl of food before him, then lifted it to his mouth, stroking his head.

Finally, she felt she knew him. Finally, she believed she could call him her own. Not as a pet, but as something wild that had chosen to be hers. And with that belief came a truth: the bear might be dangerous to others, but he wasn't dangerous to her.

This truth wrapped around Rose like a quilt, a kind of safety she hadn't felt since her father had gone.

CHAPTER 15
The Ones Who Go Missing

After nearly a month of feasts and blizzards and bandits, it was time for a Christmas tree.

Snow and Rose found a little fir near the cottage and cut it down themselves. Their tree was small, but it made the cottage smell as if the forest had come inside.

On Christmas morning, the family gathered near the fire to exchange their gifts. Rose had knitted a pretty scarf for her mother and a pale blue cap for Snow. Rose's knitting was much improved since the lumpy-scarf disaster of Snow's birthday, and the few tangled stitches here and there only added to the charm.

Their mother had made them each a new nightgown

and socks. There was a book about pirates for Snow and a brass compass for Rose. In their stockings were pieces of maple candy, wrapped in waxed paper, and fresh boxes of colored pencils. Earl Grey and the kittens got a tin of sardines.

Rose settled in with her back against the bear, as if he were a warm sofa made of fur. The fire burned bright. Snow played them her present: a song she'd been practicing off by herself, that she'd found in her old lesson books. The low, lilting sound of the bow on the strings floated up to the cedar beams of the cottage. The audience of two clapped as if they had two dozen hands.

Their mother brought out a tray of brown eggs and mugs of hot cocoa and thick slices of cinnamon bread for breakfast.

"I wish Papa were here," Snow said, looking up at the portrait that hung near the fireplace.

"He's with us," her mother said. Her eyes hung on the painting she'd made years ago.

Rose tried not to look at the portrait very often. It hurt like a window to a place she couldn't visit. But she glanced up now, smiling at the way her father's eyes sparkled like the chain of his watch that shone in his painted pocket. She'd felt so proud when they gave him that watch, with the golden circle at the back engraved

From Snow & Rose. Rose shivered and warmed her hands on her mug.

After breakfast and gifts, they dressed warmly to pay a surprise visit to Ivo's house. When they opened the cottage door, the bear struggled to his feet and attempted to step outside along with them, looking at his three humans hopefully.

"You can't come," Snow said. "We can't chance it."

When they tried to shut the door, he poked his nose out, blocking it.

Rose shook her head. "You're a wanted bear." She hugged him around the neck and locked him safely inside.

Then they set off to Ivo's house, carrying a basket of gifts.

"I wonder where bandits spend Christmas," Snow whispered to Rose as they walked with their mother.

Rose whispered back, "Wherever they can ruin it."

They passed the thicket they had searched with Ivo on the night of the feast. The blackberry brambles were covered in snow. Against the white, hidden deep in the brambles, both sisters saw something red. Something the snow had shown them that they hadn't seen before.

They padded closer to investigate and called for

their mother to wait. Snow crawled in, emerging with the red thing. She held it, dirty and tattered in the sunlight, before silently giving it to her mother.

"Papa's blanket," Rose breathed.

Their mother wore the look of someone who has lost something and found something in the same instant. She shook the layer of ice and forest from the blanket, revealing bare places where birds had pulled threads for their nests. The wool came apart in her hands, and she knelt and hugged the girls close to her, so close there was no empty space.

Snow's voice came in a muffled whisper from somewhere inside: "Mama . . . please . . . you . . . are . . . squeezing me to death."

They walked in silence until they came to a familiar plume of smoke drifting out of the earth.

The girls kicked aside a layer of snow to find the door in the ground, and then they knocked. After a few moments, Ivo's mother opened the door part of the way, peering out from her place on the stairs.

They greeted her with a "Merry Christmas!"

Ivo's mother did not look merry. She glanced around them nervously. "Come inside," she said. "And bolt the door." She turned and led them down the stairs into the main room. A dim fire burned. The big table from the feast stood empty.

"Can I offer you anything, then?" Ivo's mother asked. There was a coldness in her voice.

They stood close to the fire. Ivo's father sat still as a stone on the hearth before the walls of winding roots. He didn't even look up.

Rose and Snow looked at their mother, not sure what they should do. Rose started to unpack the basket. In the silence, their mother said, "We brought a few gifts. . . ."

They unpacked two jars of jam tied with ribbon, and then two little parcels, each with a label that read *Ivo* in Snow's and Rose's handwriting, respectively.

"We brought the jam for you," Snow said, presenting Ivo's mother with the blackberry-colored jars. "We made it."

"And these are for Ivo," Rose said, holding the two lumpy little packages, each knotted with a bow on the front. She looked around, wondering why he hadn't heard their voices. "Where is he?"

Ivo's mother took the gifts and sank into a chair, looking up at them with suspicion. "Why didn't you answer the door?"

Snow, Rose, and Edith looked back at her, confused.

"When my brother called on you." Ivo's father finally spoke, and his voice was harsh. "When the storm broke."

They sat down in a row on a wooden bench.

"Wh-why . . . ," Rose stammered.

Her mother put a hand on Snow's shoulder and finished her question. "Why did he call?"

Ivo's mother looked at the visitors, her face crumbling. "You don't know, then?" The story tumbled out: how Ivo had left the night of the feast; how their son, their only child, had never come back.

The sting of the words settled and spread. Snow and Rose sat on the hard bench, silent. "And it was just before the storm set in?" Edith said, her voice hushed.

"If it were kinder weather"—Ivo's mother looked down at her lap—"then we'd have more reason to hope."

Edith stood and went to Ivo's mother, taking her hand.

"We've been searching and searching." Ivo's mother sniffed. "But it was that King Bear, I know it. Osprey is offering a handsome reward, and he's got word to every man he knows."

"We know you've had your own go missing," Ivo's father said, standing. He went to the long table and returned with a piece of paper. "He's here." He handed Edith the paper. "With all the others."

The list held the names of everyone the woods had

taken, everyone who had never come home, scrawled in pencil. So many names that they filled the front and continued on the back: noblemen and bandits, fathers and mothers, sons and daughters.

"Why?" Edith asked, quietly breaking the silence.

Ivo's father sat back down again. He turned away, speaking into the fire, words so familiar to everyone there. "We just . . . don't . . . know."

X X X

That night, back at the cottage, their mother had two more gifts waiting beneath the tree.

"Your father and I were going to give these to you when you were older," she said. The words hung in the air as the girls opened the little boxes. Inside were necklaces, perfect in their simplicity, each a single gem suspended on a delicate gold chain.

For Snow, a freshwater pearl.

For Rose, a ruby, like a faceted petal.

"They're beautiful," Snow said, and Rose nodded. Even as they thanked their mother for their beautiful gifts, they moved slowly and spoke low and soft. The news about Ivo made everything feel muffled, as though they were moving and speaking underwater.

Snow and Rose put on the necklaces with their new

nightgowns and climbed into bed. After their mother kissed them good night, she went down to the hearth and curled up with Earl Grey, watching the sleeping bear and the dimming fire.

Snow spoke into the darkness. "Why does everyone go missing?"

Rose's voice was small when she replied: "I don't know." She paused. "What did you give to Ivo?"

Snow sighed. "That little brass elephant he liked so much. What about you?"

Rose turned over, curling her knees into her chest. "You know how he wore those old socks on his hands?"

The dark was silent.

"Mittens," Snow said.

Rose could hear tears in her sister's voice. She felt her own tears roll down her cheeks.

Outside, snow was falling again. The trees shivered like they were restless.

CHAPTER 16
The Wilds of Spring

Snow and Rose waited for news, any news, of Ivo. No news came.

Winter passed, long and dark, and the wind howled through the walls of the cottage. Snow and Rose stayed close to the fire, or the sleeping bear, their breathing radiator, to keep warm. It was cold all the time, so cold that Rose's hand would stiffen while she worked on her knitting or turned the page of a book. Snow's fingers went numb drawing wolves and little people with wings.

The same uneasy dream returned to Rose night after night: a dream of trees, surrounding her like the shifting walls of an endless house.

The girls waited the dark winter away, watching the cupboard empty and the kittens turn to cats.

Their mother prepared for the spring Equinox Market, hoping to sell a few things along with her shopping.

In March, the days inched a little longer. The sun, which seemed as if it were never coming back, returned. The snow melted. The wind died down, and the air began to warm. Outside, everything that grows began to awaken and unfurl, tender leaves on black branches and green tendrils pushing up through the blanket of dark earth.

Then, on the first day of spring, the bear was gone. He left as suddenly as he'd come, in the early hours of the dawn.

Rose wasn't awake to see him go or to hug him goodbye. She came to the breakfast table and found Snow and her mother waiting in the quiet.

Rose's hands began to worry at her sides. Before a word was said, she sensed it: an empty expanse where there should have been something warm and dark and bear-shaped.

"I didn't want to wake you," her mother said. "He was waiting at the door before the sun came up."

The sting of it hit Rose so fiercely that her ears began to hum. "And you just let him go? Out with the traps and arrows? Out where they want to kill him?"

"If an animal wants to go . . . he goes," her mother said, shrugging. "We couldn't keep him here forever." She set another place at the table. "And we couldn't *feed* him forever." Her mother eyed the empty cupboard. "Not to mention, I'll be buying a new chicken at the market." She sighed as she scraped butter onto a piece of brown toast. "It seems he ate Goldie the Second on his way out."

Rose's eyes darted to Snow, who nodded and put her head down on the table.

Their mother looked at them. "And since we no longer have a guard bear, I need you to take good care of each other the two days I'm at the market. Keep the door locked. And *no* venturing out into the woods. I wouldn't want . . ."

Rose automatically began to help her mother pack, but her eyebrows were furrowed. "Someone has to look out for him. They think he *ate* Ivo, Mama."

"Come sit down," her mother said, pouring a cup of tea. "Have some breakfast. I'll finish packing."

Rose didn't sit down. She went away, back up to their bedroom.

Edith finished packing and turned to Snow. "She just needs some time." She kissed Snow on the head.

Then she called out, "Goodbye," and closed the door. The lock clicked firmly into place.

Rose came back fully dressed, her boots laced up, but her hair was wild and unbrushed. "You could've woken me," she said to Snow in a quiet voice that held back a storm of words.

Snow looked up from her ripped piece of toast. Before she could say anything, the door had slammed. Rose was gone, out after the bear, outside into the new spring.

He can't have gone far, Rose thought. *Not yet.* Her head buzzed with thoughts of the Huntsman and the bandits and everything else in the greedy woods. The woods had taken so much already. It didn't occur to her that she could be taken, too.

Rose didn't know where she was going, but for the first time, she understood what Snow must have felt so often. But Rose had no practice fighting off the fury that wanted to overtake her.

The string inside Rose, so neatly tied, had broken.

She tore through the woods, ripping at branches, crushing ferns and mushrooms and leaves and early flowers under her boots. She stomped and kicked through the trees like a rampaging giant in one of Snow's fairy tales.

The shadows moved across the trees, and morning gave way to noon. Rose got out of the woods, out into the sunlight, at Snow's place on the hillside. In her exhaustion, she didn't listen, didn't care if bandits were there. She collapsed on the soft, new grass and she wept. She cried for her loneliness and how tentative and afraid she had been all her life. For what could happen to the bear, and for Ivo and her papa, for all those names on that list, all the people she didn't even know. She cried until she could hardly breathe.

Then Rose heard a sound, a small rustling. From the corner of her eye, she saw someone watching her.

Rose wiped her tears on her sleeve and turned. Her green eyes met two shiny ones. The big fox looked out timidly, then slowly crept closer to Rose. The only sounds were Rose's ragged breath and the whispering of the grass as the fox came toward her.

Rose sniffled and tried to calm her breathing. "Hello," she said softly.

The fox was huge, nearly the size of a wolf, but thin and narrow. Rose was almost close enough to touch its red coat. Suddenly, the fox heard something. Startled, it froze, ears perked. With a nervous leap, the fox darted away, a streak of rust-colored fur with a white tail.

Rose turned to watch it disappear into the woods.

A small, familiar white shape flickered as it left the row of dark trees.

"There you are," Snow called out. "I wondered if I'd find you here."

She came and stood next to Rose. "Days go by that I don't even think about it now," Snow said quietly, looking down at their old house. "Somehow it looks smaller than I remember." She handed a napkin-wrapped parcel to Rose and said, "I brought you something to eat."

Rose stood and dusted herself off. She ate her bread and jam gratefully as they walked.

"I can't believe you slammed the door!" Snow said, patting Rose's shoulder. "You reminded me of me."

Rose tried to muster a smile. The anger had swept through her, leaving a hollow feeling in her chest.

"What do you want to do?" Snow asked. "Since we've already broken all of Mama's rules."

"Find him," Rose answered, her voice hoarse.

Snow didn't argue. "Then it's lucky we're experts at hide-and-seek." She smiled at her sister.

"I just wish we knew where to look," Rose said.

"I think," Snow said, "we'll have to wander."

So they walked in the woods while it turned to

afternoon, looking for clues: paw prints in the earth or claw marks on the tree trunks. Any sign of the bear. They left the path and went east. They passed the library, the air around it silent, the goats' pen empty.

When they knocked at the door, nobody came. "She said she would leave," Rose said.

"I didn't believe her," Snow said, her chin on the window ledge. No signs of life showed beyond the dusty glass.

They looped back to the path and headed west.

"Look, it's the old-man trees," Snow said, pointing ahead.

The grove stretched before them, ancient branches arching overhead. They passed through the grove to a new pocket of the woods, a place where the tree trunks were soft as brown paper and wider than outstretched arms.

Rose stopped dead in her tracks and knelt down. Something dark soaked the moss and earth.

"Look," she said. She touched the ground before her and held it up to Snow. The tip of her finger was painted red.

A trail of blood ran like a red ribbon. It stopped here and there, then picked up again, staining the leaves.

"It's so much," Snow said, her voice worried.

Please, Rose wished silently as they followed. *Please let it not be him.*

Suddenly, the trail stopped. The girls hunted, shifting leaves and lifting branches, afraid to see where it ended. The hunt took them to the base of a big tree, so enormous that ten men, all together, couldn't clasp hands around it. They circled it, marveling at its size. Hidden in the smooth bark, Rose caught a glint of metal, and pointed it out to Snow. The metal belonged to brass hinges, the only hint that gave away what was camouflaged in the tree's side: a door.

At the base of the door, blood stained the ground.

"This is where it leads," Snow said. She put her ear to the door. Rose joined her, shivering with nerves. They heard nothing.

"Are we going in?" Rose asked, but she already knew the answer. Her worry for the bear was louder than everything else. She tried the doorknob. It turned, and the girls took cautious steps inside.

They walked into a round entryway, rustic but magnificent. The walls carved into the hollow tree were painted a brilliant blue. Hanging in mounted pairs, from floor to ceiling, were rows and rows of antlers and horns. Light entered overhead, and a thin beam illuminated the way forward, sloping deeper underground. Snow and Rose walked farther in, following the fresh ribbon of blood, bright as it traced the wooden floor, leading them into another room. A workshop, a trophy room.

The girls felt hundreds of eyes watching them.

They stood in the center of the room, surrounded by a silent, still menagerie. Every open space was crowded with frozen birds and glass-eyed deer; wildcats with silent, growling mouths and sharp teeth; black boars with curving tusks. Some were the size that nature would make them, but some were twice as large, the mark of the woods. The afternoon light fell weakly from windows set into the ceiling, like the ones at Ivo's house.

Snow and Rose knew who called this place home, even before they saw the blue-feathered arrow. It was still in the heart of the blackbird that lay on a dark table in the center of the room, its huge wings sprawled at inelegant angles. Its feathers shone black, then green, then blue.

"Can we go home?" Snow said quietly, looking around. The color was gone from her cheeks.

Rose stared at the dead bird. Her heart was sickened, too, but also relieved that it was not the bear. Although, as she looked at the dark, lifeless eyes of the blackbird, her relief was replaced by the thought that this bird might've meant something to someone.

It might've been *somebody's* bear. "I'm not going home," she said. She looked at the mounted heads on the wall. "Not until we find him."

Suddenly, they heard a door open and shut. The sound of deep voices came closer. The girls ran from the worktable and hid among the lifeless feathers and fur, as quiet as the silent animals. The sound of the Huntsman's voice was joined by several other men's.

"To the east," one said. "That's where he was seen."

Rose and Snow peered over an elk's back.

The Huntsman appeared, doling out cups and pouring drinks. "I know you boys don't like to come this far in," he said. The girls recognized the ramshackle military coats and the men who wore them: two bandits. "But I'll make it worth your while."

"We'll need to see that reward, as agreed," one bandit said, eyeing the Huntsman. He chuckled. "We nearly had him, only a few months back. Lucky for us, now you've tripled the ransom."

"Nothing lucky in what happened," the Huntsman growled. "I loved that boy like my own." Snow and Rose looked at each other, hearing the sorrow that hid below his growl. The Huntsman tossed a leather pouch onto the table, and it clinked with heavy coins.

"Monster of a blackbird," the other bandit said as he traced the feathers with his finger.

The Huntsman gathered provisions from drawers and cupboards and stuffed them into his hunting bag. "Remember," he said. "The reward is yours if you bring him to me. But if we come upon him together"—he shouldered his bow—"the bear is mine."

CHAPTER 17
Adventurers

The girls held their breath as the men finished collecting their things. When they heard the door close, Rose and Snow waited another moment to be sure the men were gone. Then they quickly made their way from the Huntsman's house toward their own cottage.

"We need supplies," Rose said, her voice frantic. She walked quickly. "We need the compass to know where east is. We need blankets, food . . ."

"How long are we going out to look?" Snow said, worry in her voice.

"If you don't want to go, you don't have to," Rose said. "You can stay."

"But—what are we going to do if we find him?" Snow asked.

"I don't really know," Rose said.

"I'll go," Snow said. Rose's stillness had broken, and Snow saw everything beneath it. She couldn't make her go alone.

"We can look until the sun goes down," Rose said. "If we have to, we can set up camp."

When they reached the cottage, they gathered their things. Snow fed the cats, and Rose rummaged through shelves and cupboards, filling her satchel with a flask of water, a bit of food, her notebook, the compass, her father's knife, and the sparking stones.

"Just in case," Rose said, handing a lantern to Snow. Snow grumbled as she slung it over her arm. Rose rolled up two quilts. Snow eyed them suspiciously, and Rose repeated, "Just in case." She handed a quilt to Snow, and they each threw a bundle over one shoulder. Then they headed east.

X X X

The forest was unseasonably warm as the girls walked, now moving more slowly. They followed the compass arrow deeper into the east woods than they had ever been before. They walked side by side as bars of sun glowed warm behind the budding trees.

Rose kept the compass in her hand and led them, driven by a sense of purpose. She felt exhilarated as they wound their way through new trees. They had come to an unfamiliar part of the forest. Every once in a while, Rose would stop and make a note of a landmark, such as a big rock that looked like a giant hand pointing at the sky, or a clearing of wild violets. Snow followed dutifully, weighed down with provisions. Each new, unexplored bend held the hope of finding him. They walked farther and farther, searching for any sign of the bear. They found a flower that looked like a ballet slipper, a small bone, a brilliant blue feather as long as Snow's arm, but no trace of him.

The trees unfolded before them, the bare spring arms waving them on, leading them away from rough ground and hidden ditches. Rose made a note of a bogland as they skirted around its dank smell and black mud. Luckily, they crossed paths with no bandits. Unluckily, they crossed paths with no bears.

When the sun began to sink in the sky, Snow and Rose stopped to rest in a place where a small waterfall gathered into a clear, cold pool. The water ran from the falls and disappeared into a stream that continued hidden underground. They unlaced their boots to rest their feet on the cool earth. Rose pulled their father's knife from her satchel and cut an apple into two halves, handing one to Snow. They sat to eat on rocks that rose up in a ring around the pool, cushioned with moss.

Snow put down her lantern and bundle beside her rock, at the base of an old stump, not guessing that it was a home. Then the girls heard a hum. They looked around as the hum grew louder. Suddenly, the bees appeared, billowing from the stump like furious smoke.

"Crumbs!" Snow shrieked, leaping up. She waded, splashing into the water, clothes and all.

Rose clambered up onto a rock that jutted out of the pool. She watched as the swarm hovered over Snow, who gulped a breath and ducked under. The bees began to scatter, but Snow stayed under. As Rose watched the water for Snow, she felt a sting. She swatted at the air, and Rose felt her satchel slip.

She grasped for the leather strap just as the satchel fell to the rock.

The bag opened, its contents tumbling out into the water: the bread she had packed, the sparking stones, and finally the compass. The current pulled them, rushing toward the hidden stream.

Snow's head emerged, and she was gasping for breath. She waded waist-deep, fishing for the compass with frantic hands. Snow rescued the compass, but it was filled with water. The arrow didn't point anywhere.

They climbed back to the bank of the waterfall,

Snow's wet clothes clinging, both girls shivering. As she handed Rose the broken compass, Rose noticed that something was missing from around Snow's neck.

Snow followed Rose's eyes. Her hand went to her neck, and she realized that her necklace was gone.

Snow's eyes filled with tears that were quickly replaced by a scowl. "I want to go home," she said. "I knew this was a bad idea."

"Oh, Snow . . . I'm sorry," Rose said. Guilt swept through her as she wrapped a dry quilt around her sister. She thought of the pearl somewhere beneath the water, lost forever. "What . . . what about the bear?"

"What about *us*?" Snow asked.

Rose put on her boots silently.

"Whatever took Ivo could take us, too," Snow continued, peeling off her wet stockings.

Rose looked around at the endless forest. The light was starting to fade. Nothing looked familiar or safe. Worrying about the bear had taken up so much room, she hadn't thought to worry about *them*. Not until now.

"I want to go home," Snow said again. Then, looking up and seeing Rose's face, Snow sighed, shaking her head. "Do you really think we can save him?"

Rose handed Snow her boots. "We're the only ones who *want* to save him."

They passed through a grove of thin white birches,

but their searching was slow and fraught. Snow grumbled, shivering in her wet clothes. Rose was afraid to wander much farther without the compass. She could hear her stomach growl above Snow's grumbling, and her feet ached.

When night began to fall, they found a clearing. Snow barely spoke as they laid their quilts out on the ground and placed the lantern between them. She walked off to gather a small pile of kindling to build a fire. She returned to their campsite. "Sparking stones," Snow requested, her voice quiet and flat.

"They . . . ," Rose trailed off.

"They fell in, too," Snow said. She threw the wood down. "So we freeze."

Rose fished a small piece of cheese and a single damp roll from her satchel. She took their father's knife from its secure pocket and made two meager sandwiches. She offered one to Snow.

Snow ate silently, looking at the ground. Her paleness glowed in the half light. "We're going back in the morning, I hope you know."

"I'm sorry about your necklace," Rose said, helpless at how little the words could do. She sighed and looked up, searching for the hidden moon. "I just thought . . ." Her shoulders fell. "We couldn't save Papa."

Snow didn't say anything.

The warmth of the day had gone with the sun, and the night was turning cold. Rose paused, trying to find the right words. "I thought we could save . . . someone."

"Papa will come back," Snow said. "I believe it."

Rose breathed in and shook her head. Suddenly, words tumbled out so fast she couldn't stop them. "He's gone, Snow! And he's never coming back."

In the horrible silence, Rose wanted to un-say the words. But even if she could, it wouldn't make them any less true.

Snow stared at Rose, stunned. Then she looked away again.

The night passed without another word, just the sounds of owls and night birds and the flapping of bat wings as they flocked overhead.

X X X

"I have told you that you cannot make it happen," said the old one.

"But they are lost," said the young one.

"If it is supposed to happen, it will happen," said the old one in a voice that shook every branch of every tree.

"But I can help them find their way," said the young one.

"I have told you—" Before the old one could finish, however, the young one was gone.

X X X

In the morning, things looked even more unfamiliar. Like the shifting woods in Rose's dream, the walls of trees seemed to have moved around them while they slept.

"I think it's this way," Rose said, walking slowly in one direction. Snow followed along, but then Rose stopped. Her cheeks blushed hot with shame. Just yesterday, she had been a real explorer. She'd sailed on her sense of certainty and purpose, and today, in the cold morning, she had crashed them into the rocks.

"Can't you tell anything by whatever you were writing down?" Snow asked. Her stomach growled.

"I don't know," Rose said. They had gone too far. Her mind was clouded with doubt. Rose folded and unfolded her paper, looking at her little drawings of the stone hand and the violet patch and the paths she thought they had taken. Without the compass, it all meant nothing. She pictured the magnificent maps in her favorite book and crumpled the useless paper in her fist.

Snow sat down on the ground and started to cry. "This is your fault," she said. "I'm starving. . . . My necklace . . . And we're really lost!"

Rose looked out at the endless forest and lifted her face to the patches of sky cut through by the black branches overhead.

Adventurers

"You didn't *have* to come," Rose muttered. But she knew she wouldn't have gone without Snow. Because she needed her. Because she was Rose, the rabbit-hearted.

"Will someone please help us?!" Snow called out to nobody. The only answer was the wind, ruffling the ferns and blowing more tangles into her hair.

"I'll find the way," Rose said, trying to sound confident. "Come on, get up."

"I'm cold." Snow sniffed and wiped her nose.

"You can wear my sweater," Rose said.

"This is still your fault," Snow muttered.

They made their way into a patch of short blue-green ferns. Hundreds of little white winged insects rose up around them. The sight was so beautiful that Snow and Rose couldn't help but stop, marveling in silence.

The insects were not bees or butterflies. The sunlight filtered down in bright beams, making them glow as they bobbed and danced around the girls' shoulders.

"They're like fairies," Snow said softly.

All of a sudden, the insects gathered into one glowing creature, a small person lit from within, unfolding a pair of wings at its back. Then a bigger creature flew shimmering out of the trees. It joined the smaller one, and they hovered above the ferns on translucent wings veined in gold, as delicate as paper.

Snow's hand flew to her mouth. She looked at Rose. "I told you," she whispered. "It *is* fairies."

Rose's eyes were lit with the glow of the fairies before her, on golden wings, weightless, impossible.

The fairies beckoned to the girls. And since Snow and Rose were already lost, they followed. The fairies led the way through the woods, and as the girls went, things grew more familiar.

They walked through the white birch grove, past the waterfall, around the bogland, and through the clearing with its carpet of violets, then past the stone hand. By noon they had reached the stream where they'd fought the river monster and saved the Little Man. Snow and Rose tossed down their things and rushed to get a drink from the water.

When they turned, they saw the glow of the fairies growing smaller, receding into the trees. They were leaving.

Snow turned to Rose. "I told you I saw a fairy at Ivo's house. Now do you believe me?"

Rose was about to reply, but she was stopped by a rustling sound.

Then out of the trees, out of the very leaves themselves, the Little Man emerged. Without claws or sharp teeth or arrows or daggers, he carried his own air of menace.

The girls inched closer together.

"Oh!" he sneered. "The beard butchers. Come to butcher me again?"

The girls dropped the things they carried.

"You don't have to worry about us *saving* you again, if that's what you mean," Snow fired back.

"Didn't I say that if ever we crossed paths," the Little Man asked, "you'd be sorry, very sorry?"

"We should run," Rose murmured. Her hand went to her necklace, her fingers worrying the chain.

The Little Man's eyes flashed as they caught on the golden chain, and what he did next was impossibly quick. He grabbed the necklace and tore it from Rose's neck.

The Little Man held the delicate chain up to see it, then held it to his ears to listen to it. "Oh, lovely, civilized, darling gold." His feet danced beneath him. "They must give it." His eyes flashed. "A gift for me."

Both Snow and Rose stared in shock.

Then he turned on his heel and darted away with the quickness of the thief he was. Snow dashed after him.

"Just let him have it!" Rose called. She felt the danger that the Little Man had left in his wake.

But Snow ran with the recklessness of someone who had lost too much. She turned her head and shouted back, "We can't lose them both!"

Rose grabbed her satchel from the ground, leaving all their other things where they had fallen, and ran after Snow.

The Little Man sprang forward on his backward-bending legs, with Snow at his heels, a white ghost flashing between the trees. Rose's black hair flew behind her as she chased her sister, like the night chasing the day.

Rose fought to keep Snow and the Little Man in sight. Through the trees, she saw them come to the mouth of a cave that loomed out of the ground. Then Snow followed the Little Man into the black.

Rose arrived just in time to hear the Little Man's voice cackling five words before the entrance to the cave closed over.

Rose stood in the sudden stillness. She wasn't sure whether the words were meant for her or for Snow, only that they seemed to echo in the rocks that now stood before her.

"You are your father's daughter."

CHAPTER 18

Terrible Am I

The trees flew by, blurring as Rose ran.

She heard, every so often, a sound behind her. But it could've been just the sound of her own footfalls, for each time she turned, she found nobody there.

When she reached the library, she pounded on the door, but again no one came. She waited another moment, then flung it open.

The library was empty.

The spiral staircase stood alone. Its shelves were vacant and unkempt, the tidy labels scattered below. The only movement came from the dust that floated in stray beams of light.

Rose ran up the stairs, her eyes scanning the shelves. All she saw was bits of rubbish. That was all that was left. . . . Maybe that's all it had ever been. Her eyes caught on a little box near her feet. The box was printed with faded letters and rattled when she shook it. Rose opened it to find three matches. She remembered standing on the riverbank, the Little Man's fright at the sparking stones. How his eyes had filled with fear at the word *fire*.

She hurried to tuck the matches into her satchel. Now she had a real plan. She ran out of the library and made her way to Ivo's farm.

Rose had never run so much in her life. Her legs ached and her breath burned, but the sun was already lower in the sky. Rose hoped there was enough daylight left to get what she needed and return to the cave.

Again, she heard a rustling behind her. Again, she turned to find nobody there.

At Ivo's farm, she knocked and called out, but like at the library, nobody came. Rose found the hidden lever in the tree. She could barely pull it. As the door in the ground opened and she stepped down the stairs, she remembered the first time she and Snow had come. She remembered tumbling in, and Ivo's face when he'd found them.

She reached the mushroom caverns and called out

again. Rose looked up at the walls, lit by the dim lantern moss, but they were empty. She couldn't see a single mushroom.

Then she realized why the cavern was so bare. "Of course," she remembered. "The market." Near the back of the ledges, she noticed a few mushrooms still growing in the dark.

But Rose was looking for one particular mushroom.

She found the ledge she was looking for and stood on her tiptoes. She reached up, feeling around blindly until her hand grazed something round and hollow. Then she felt another, then another.

It was the first sign of hope in days. Three Sandman's Pockets would be enough to make the Little Man sleep for a long time.

She placed them gently, like precious eggs, beside the matches and the ivory handle of her father's knife: a small but dangerous arsenal.

As Rose climbed back into the sunlight, she filled her lungs with the smell of spring. It came from every hidden root unwinding, from everything that fought its way out of the ground. Rose retraced her way back to the cave and back to Snow. "You are your father's daughter," she told herself over and over again as she ran, and the words made her brave.

When Rose reached the cave, she heard the

mysterious rustling again. She held her breath. Then she caught a glimpse of a narrow snout, a flash of red fur, and a white-tipped tail.

"It's just you!" she said, breathing out.

The big red fox came toward Rose on tentative paws.

"Can you help me?" she asked, eyeing the rocks that blocked the entrance to the cave.

She knelt down to feel the stones, cemented in moss that held fast. Everything was solid, fixed, immovable. The red fox sniffed at the seams in the rock.

"If there isn't a way *through*, the only way in"—she looked at the fox, which had busied itself at the base of the entrance—"is under."

The fox was already burrowing. Rose's hands didn't work nearly as well, but she helped dig. The fox made fast work of the tunnel. Its tail vanished quickly, kicking black earth behind it. When the fox returned for her, snout first, the way inside was complete.

Rose crawled in, following the fox into the dark burrow, climbing underneath and around the cave's entrance.

She stood and dusted herself off. All around her was black, but just ahead the walls glowed warm and bright. Rose gathered up her courage. She put her hand on the fox's back, and they walked through the dark cavern toward the golden chamber.

Just beyond the darkness, the cave glittered with mountains of treasure: rings and crowns and cups and coins from far-off lands, like the picture of Aladdin's cave in one of Snow's books. An opening in the cave somewhere high overhead made the gold glint with sunlight.

Rose curled up her fists and called out for Snow.

No answer came, just an echo.

Then the Little Man appeared with Snow beside him. At the sight of him, the fox bolted.

Snow was silent, but her eyes glared. Her legs didn't move; her arms stuck straight at her sides like a figurine's.

"I grew tired of her rude conversation." The Little Man sighed. "Once I showed her this . . ." The Little Man held something in his hand.

It was a watch, very like her own father's watch. *Exactly* like his watch.

Suddenly everything braided together so neatly in Rose's mind. The answer to the *why*.

"Thief!" Rose shouted. Even though she knew the answer, she cried, "Where did you get that?"

The Little Man mused aloud, taunting her. "What shall your sister become, hmm? She seems like a perfect piglet to me."

"Hold your breath, Snow!" Rose called. Quick as a

rabbit, she pulled out the first Sandman mushroom and threw it. It burst before the Little Man, cloaking him in blue smoke.

"You shouldn't have done that," he said, his voice like an eerie song. "Terrible am I."

As the smoke cleared, Rose saw him lay his hand on Snow's shoulder, whispering strange words, an ominous incantation.

Snow's body transformed instantly into a white piglet with blue eyes and a pink snout.

Rose felt as if her breath had been knocked from her chest. The piglet ran to her, squealing. Rose knelt down and put her arms around the trembling creature.

"If they will not give it, then I must take it," the Little Man said. "The ones I take from never say a word."

The piglet kicked against a small, jingling pouch of coins, nudging it toward Rose. She looked down and recognized it instantly: Ivo's coins. Rose thought of all the oversized creatures that roamed the woods. She knew why the giant blackbird and the monstrous silver fish had wanted the Little Man dead. He was more than just a thief.

"You!" Rose said, standing up in fury. "You're the Menace of the Woods!"

"I made them all." The Little Man laughed. "And

you won't tell a soul." He inched toward her. "I only have to lay a finger on you and speak the words."

Rose backed away. She held her breath and threw another mushroom, which dusted blue all around the Little Man. But he stood, unchanged, his eyes open, completely awake.

"Why don't they work?" Rose cried in frustration. The piglet flopped over at her feet with a thump.

The Little Man laughed. "Nothing of the forest made can harm me."

"But if you can change things into something else, why can't you turn *anything you want* into gold?" Rose felt in her satchel. She had to distract him. "Why do you have to steal it? And hurt the ones you steal from?"

"I work in blood and bones and wood and green," the Little Man said, his cat eyes flashing. He backed Rose into the dark tunnel, away from the sleeping piglet and the golden treasure. "Everything that grows. If you plant a coin, it doesn't grow." He clasped her father's watch. "It must be taken."

The Little Man lunged for her.

Rose was ready. She struck a match and held it before her, a flickering shield. The Little Man recoiled in fear.

The match burned down to her fingers and went out. The Little Man sprang again, but she struck another match. Rose walked backward in the dark, her heart thundering in her chest. She watched the Little Man through the flame as the second match burned down to nothing, leaving only one more.

Rose lit the last match, and her heart sank as it burned down. She let it bite her fingers before turning to smoke in the dark of the tunnel. Now Rose had only one defense left.

The two circled each other, Rose's eyes locked on the eyes of a creature she couldn't understand, that defied all reason.

She wiped her tears on her sleeve and took her father's knife from the satchel.

"Oh, come now. Be reasonable," the Little Man said in a voice of false politeness.

Rose held the knife to his chest. "There is no reason here."

"You wouldn't dare, child," the Little Man said, laughing at her fear.

"Wouldn't I?" Rose said. The knife shook in her hand.

Then the mouth of the cavern opened; rocks trembled and fell. Light flooded the cavern, and a shadow appeared.

CHAPTER 19
The Bear Returns

Like a black mountain chain come alive stood the shadow of the bear.

Rose saw him, and her heart leapt.

The bear let out a low, menacing growl. The ground shook, and the cave walls shuddered. Fear flashed across the Little Man's face as he turned from Rose, but she held her knife steady. The bear advanced toward them.

The Little Man lunged and knocked the knife from her hand, then wielded it as his own weapon against the bear.

At this, the bear roared and the Little Man fell

back as another rumble began. The golden mountains heaped behind them began to tumble to the ground, all the treasures of a hundred years' thieving and hoarding, everything taken from those who went walking in the woods and never came home.

The Little Man scrambled back to his gold, frantically stuffing his pockets with jewels and grasping at coins, as if he could escape with a sliver of his fortune. The stone walls of the cave shook all around them.

Rose grabbed the white piglet, heaving its drowsy weight in her arms. She staggered toward the mouth of the cavern as the bear rose to his feet behind her, a fierce tower. His claws tore the air, and his teeth flashed.

Then a final roar came.

Rose hurried to the light at the entrance the bear had forced open. She saw the fox outside, watching from between the trees. She heard the sound of crashing metal behind her, of coins and golden things falling.

The bear thundered out behind her. Safe outside, they turned just in time to see the final collapse, from a distance, like a diorama in a small box. The Little Man clutched at his gold, and it spilled from his hands. He wouldn't abandon his treasures even as the cave around him shook. The walls themselves were shedding stones now, falling and crashing, so that they soon blocked the way into the cave. Just before they did, Rose saw what became of the Little Man.

He was buried in the avalanche of his own stolen mountains.

The bear made a noise like a great sigh, and then he collapsed a few yards away. But Rose had to take care of Snow.

She laid the piglet down on the soft moss and leaves of the ground, and the creature began to awaken. It blinked its pale blue eyes, and slowly something began to happen.

The piglet became Snow once again. The Little Man's enchantment was broken.

Rose squeezed her fiercely. From somewhere inside the hug, Snow grumbled, and Rose knew she was really and truly her sister.

The bear's breath was ragged in the quiet, and they hurried to their feet. The girls ran to the bear's side, but he was fearfully diminished, worse than they had ever seen him before.

Rose clasped her arms around his neck, and Snow leaned her ear to his chest and listened for his heartbeat. But as they clutched his fur, his body, once so impossibly sturdy, began to sag beneath their embrace. They felt him shrink. They felt him disappear until it seemed they'd wrapped their arms around an old fur coat.

As the fur fell away, they both closed their eyes. They were afraid to open them, afraid to see what was left.

But then they heard a voice. It was a ghost's voice, and it said, "My only Snow. My only Rose."

They both opened their eyes, and there, as if no time had passed, stood their own father, back from death.

"You loved me even as a beast," he said, his eyes kind as the bear's eyes. "In the lonely spell, your love gave me strength." He gathered them in his arms.

"It was you." Rose heard the words without commanding her voice. "But why did you leave the cottage?"

Their father looked down. He tucked Rose's hair behind her ear. "I couldn't stay with you any longer, not like that."

"But how did you find us again?" Snow said, grasping her father's hands in her own.

"The fox led me," he said, looking around but not finding what his eyes sought. "He was just here—"

The girls looked behind their father to see not an overgrown fox but Ivo racing through the trees on skinny legs.

"The fox was Ivo!" Rose explained, smiling up at their father.

The girls called out to him, and Ivo paused for a moment to look back, but they knew he couldn't stay.

He smiled and gave a triumphant wave before bounding off in the direction of his house. Rose hoped that his family would be home from the market, that they waited for him underground.

"And you ate Goldie the Second . . . ," Snow scolded, shaking her head.

Their father shrugged and smiled an apology. Snow laughed and reached up to tousle his hair.

But Rose just stared at him, so grateful to be wrong. She touched his face, feeling it warm and familiar beneath her fingers, holding it in her hands as if it would vanish any minute. They stood there in this moment, the last of the day's light streaming through the trees, falling warm around them.

"It's time to go home." Their father put his arms around them, Snow on one side, Rose on the other. He held them close as they walked, and in his steps, Rose felt the slightest trace of a limp.

The three were so giddy with happiness that they barely noticed the others. All around them, the forest was filled with the others who had been lost, others who were changed, too.

The spell that held them captive was broken, and they turned from birds and beasts back into who they once were. All the people the woods had taken, all the fathers and sons and mothers and daughters—it had given them back.

A feeling of celebration spread through the woods as the changed ones found their long-forgotten voices. Little glowing lights danced in the air above them, weaving their way through the new leaves. Dozens of feet took dozens of different paths, but each heart beat with the same four words: *You are going home.*

On their own way, Snow and Rose saw their mother. She ran to them, marveling, unable to speak. Then three became four. As they walked between the trees, under victorious branches, their warm arms held each other tight, whole again.

And the ending of that story is the beginning of a different story altogether. . . .